#6

MY BOYFRIEND IS A MONSTER
Wrapped Up in You

OR

MUMMY CAN'T BUY ME LOVE

OR

MUMMY DEAREST

OR

TRUE LOVE WAITS FIVE HUNDRED YEARS

OR

A RUN FOR HER MUMMY

OR

LOVE INCAN-TATION

OR

HOW TO PRESERVE A RELATIONSHIP

DAN JOLLEY

Illustrated by NATALIE NOURIGAT

GRAPHIC UNIVERSE™ · MINNEAPOLIS · NEW YORK

STORY BY
DAN JOLLEY

ILLUSTRATIONS BY
NATALIE NOURIGAT

LETTERING BY
GRACE LU

COVER COLORING BY
JENN MANLEY LEE

Graphic Universe™
A division of Lerner Publishing Group, Inc.
241 First Avenue North
Minneapolis, MN 55401 U.S.A.

Website address: www.lernerbooks.com

Main body text set in CCWildwords. Typeface provided by Comicraft Design.

Library of Congress Cataloging-in-Publication Data

Jolley, Dan.
    Wrapped up in you / by Dan Jolley ; illustrated by Natalie Nourigat.
        p.   cm. — (My boyfriend is a monster; #6)
    Summary: North Carolina eighteen-year-old Staci tries to keep her friend Faith safe from a group of witches but winds up helping the Incan mummy the group has reanimated, who also happens to be very attractive and charming.
    ISBN: 978-0-7613-6856-4 (lib. bdg. : alk. paper)
    1. Graphic novels. [1. Graphic novels. 2. Horror stories. 3. Mummies—Fiction. 4. Witches—Fiction.
5. North Carolina—Fiction.] I. Nourigat, Natalie, ill. II. Title.
PZ7.7.J65Wr 2012
741.5'973—dc23   2011044655

Manufactured in the United States of America
1 – PP – 7/15/12

CHAPTER ONE

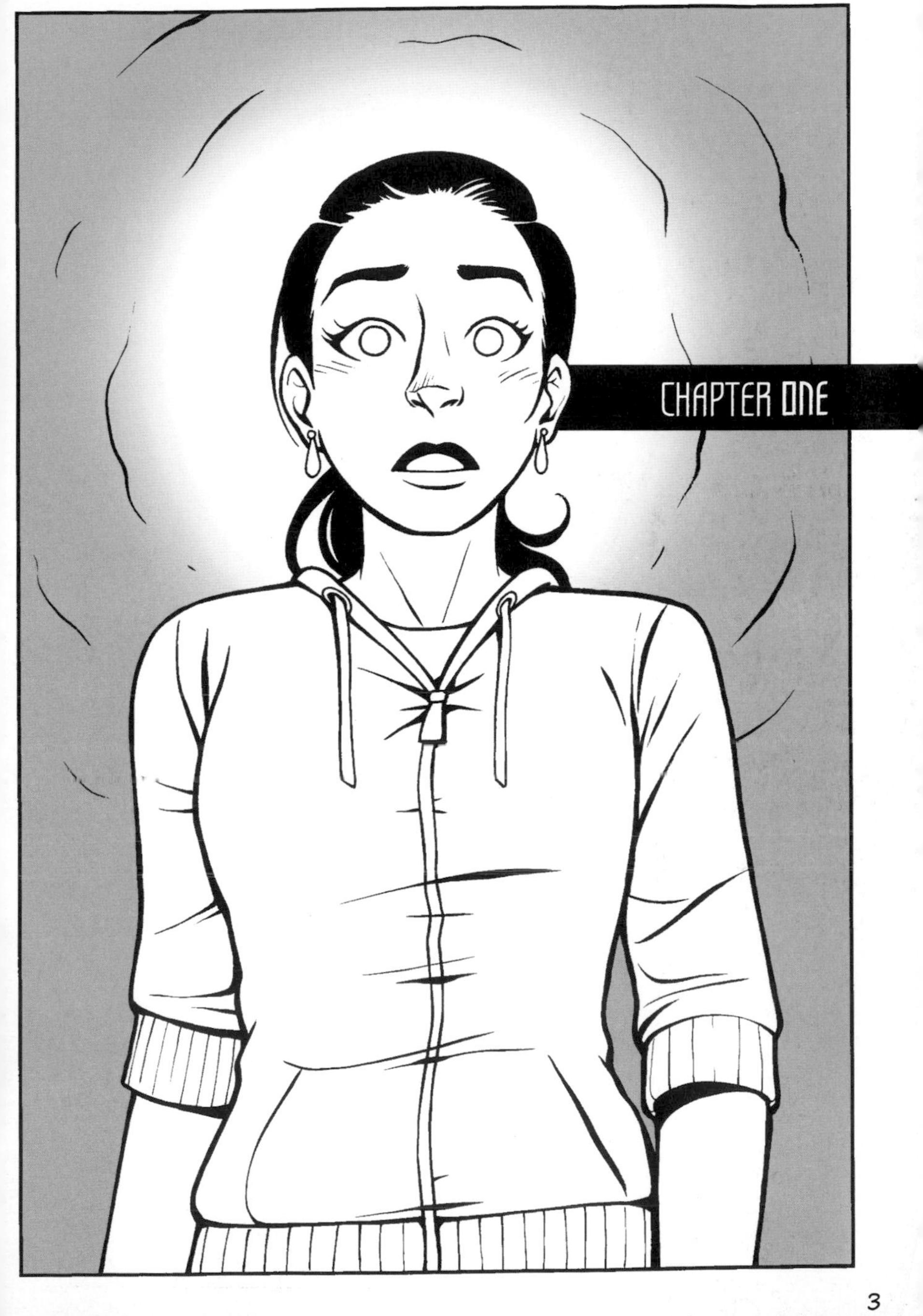

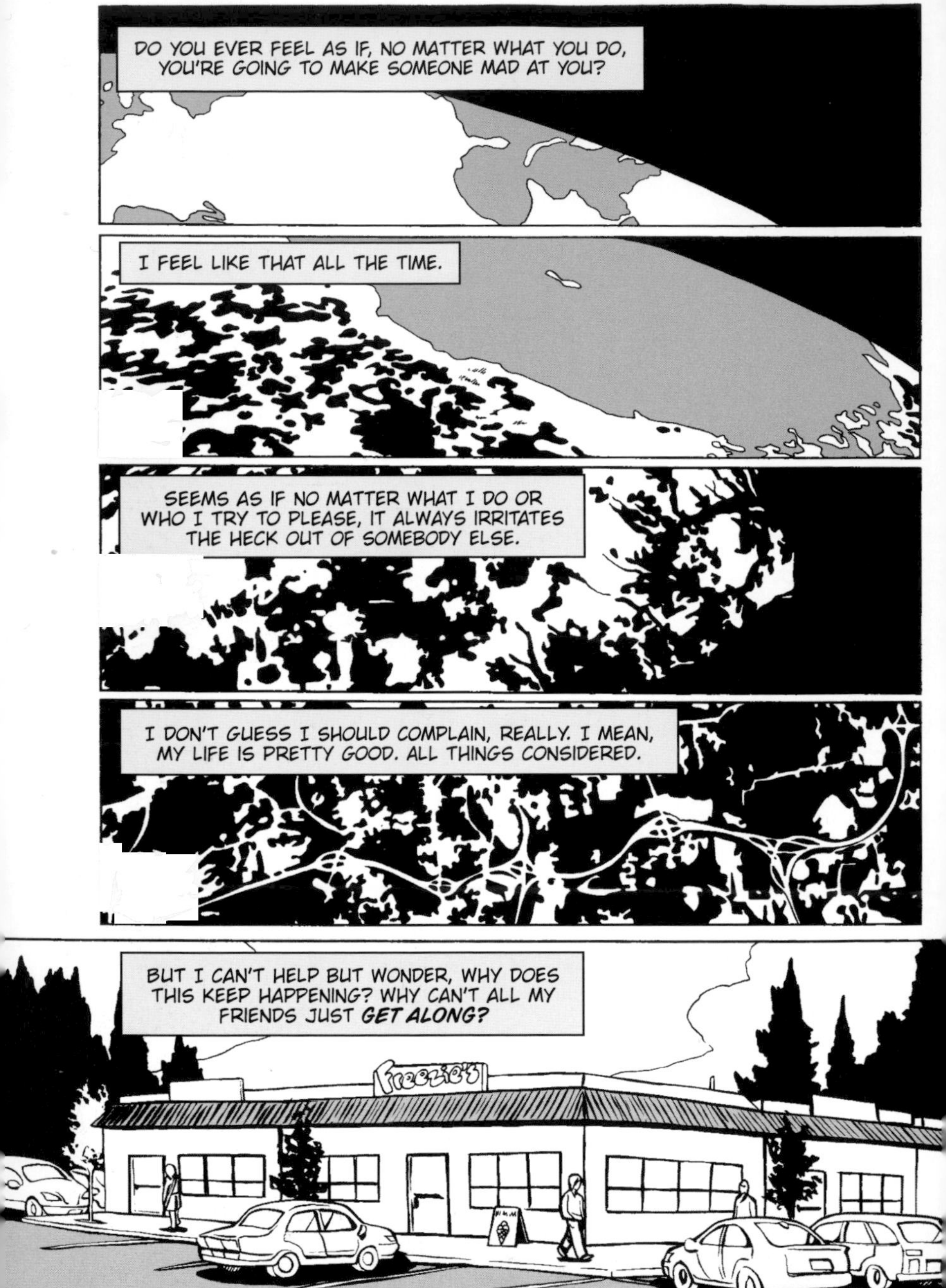
DO YOU EVER FEEL AS IF, NO MATTER WHAT YOU DO, YOU'RE GOING TO MAKE SOMEONE MAD AT YOU?
I FEEL LIKE THAT ALL THE TIME.
SEEMS AS IF NO MATTER WHAT I DO OR WHO I TRY TO PLEASE, IT ALWAYS IRRITATES THE HECK OUT OF SOMEBODY ELSE.
I DON'T GUESS I SHOULD COMPLAIN, REALLY. I MEAN, MY LIFE IS PRETTY GOOD. ALL THINGS CONSIDERED.
BUT I CAN'T HELP BUT WONDER, WHY DOES THIS KEEP HAPPENING? WHY CAN'T ALL MY FRIENDS JUST GET ALONG?
Freezie's

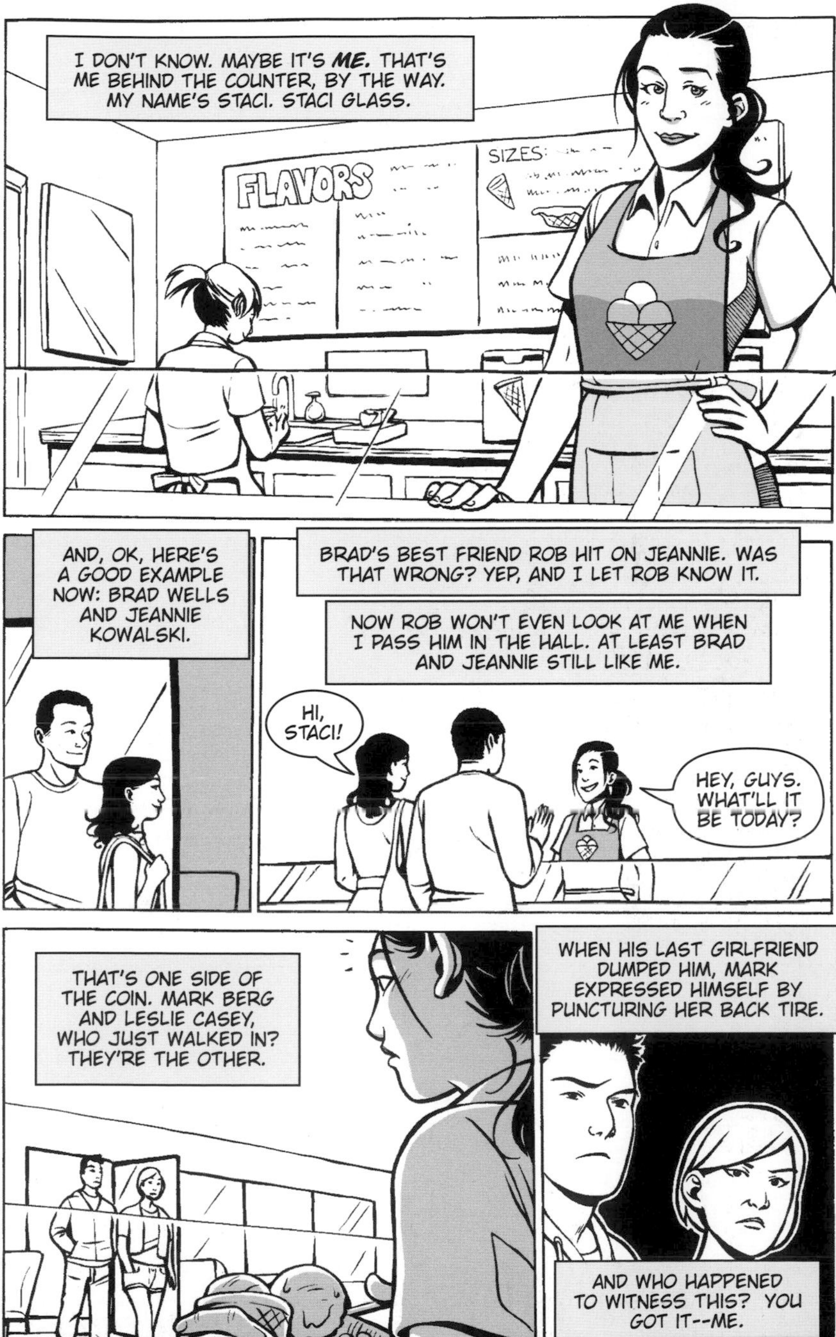
I DON'T KNOW. MAYBE IT'S ME. THAT'S ME BEHIND THE COUNTER, BY THE WAY. MY NAME'S STACI. STACI GLASS.
FLAVORS
SIZES:
AND, OK, HERE'S A GOOD EXAMPLE NOW: BRAD WELLS AND JEANNIE KOWALSKI.
BRAD'S BEST FRIEND ROB HIT ON JEANNIE. WAS THAT WRONG? YEP, AND I LET ROB KNOW IT.
NOW ROB WON'T EVEN LOOK AT ME WHEN I PASS HIM IN THE HALL. AT LEAST BRAD AND JEANNIE STILL LIKE ME.
HI, STACI!
HEY, GUYS. WHAT'LL IT BE TODAY?
THAT'S ONE SIDE OF THE COIN. MARK BERG AND LESLIE CASEY, WHO JUST WALKED IN? THEY'RE THE OTHER.
WHEN HIS LAST GIRLFRIEND DUMPED HIM, MARK EXPRESSED HIMSELF BY PUNCTURING HER BACK TIRE.
AND WHO HAPPENED TO WITNESS THIS? YOU GOT IT--ME.

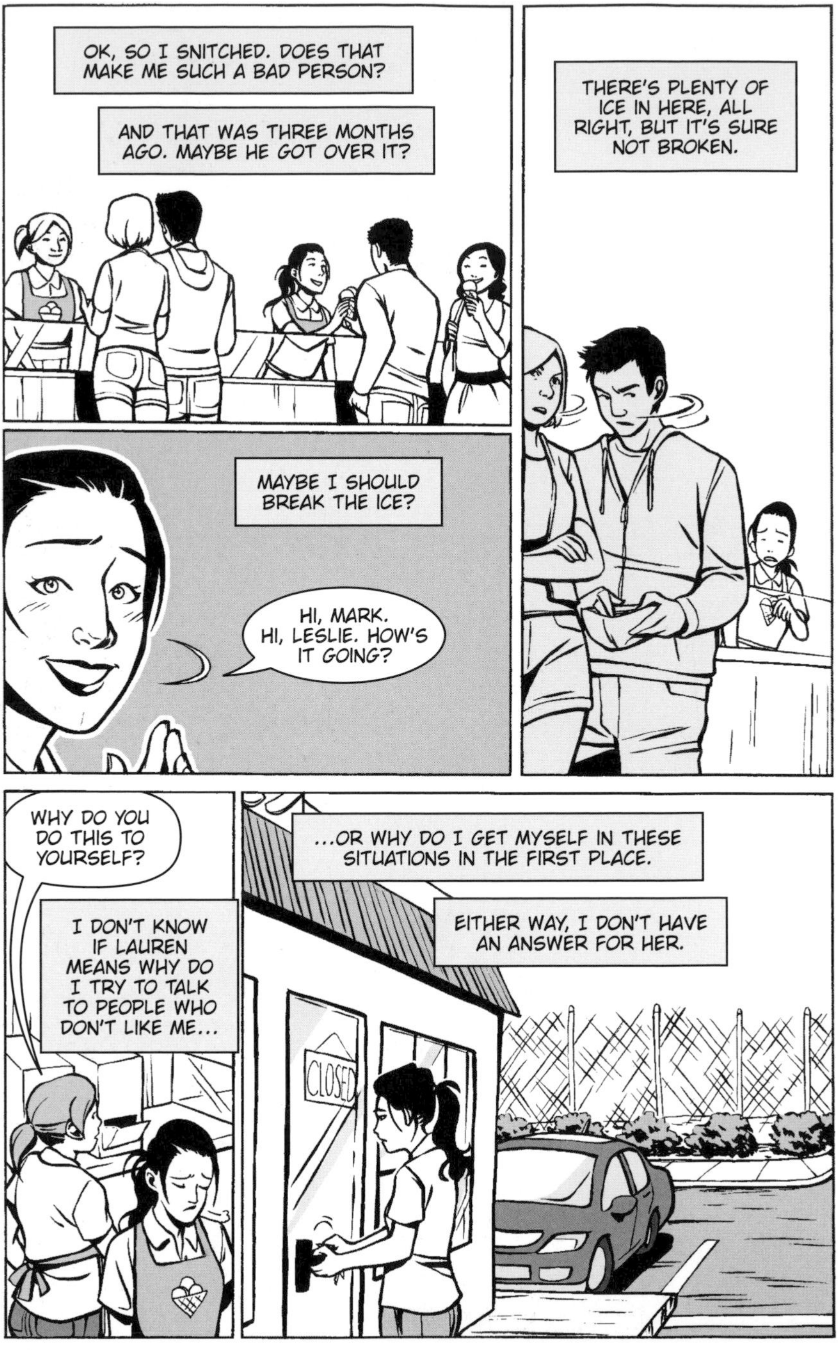
OK, SO I SNITCHED. DOES THAT MAKE ME SUCH A BAD PERSON?
AND THAT WAS THREE MONTHS AGO. MAYBE HE GOT OVER IT?
THERE'S PLENTY OF ICE IN HERE, ALL RIGHT, BUT IT'S SURE NOT BROKEN.
MAYBE I SHOULD BREAK THE ICE?
HI, MARK. HI, LESLIE. HOW'S IT GOING?
WHY DO YOU DO THIS TO YOURSELF?
I DON'T KNOW IF LAUREN MEANS WHY DO I TRY TO TALK TO PEOPLE WHO DON'T LIKE ME...
...OR WHY DO I GET MYSELF IN THESE SITUATIONS IN THE FIRST PLACE.
EITHER WAY, I DON'T HAVE AN ANSWER FOR HER.
CLOSED

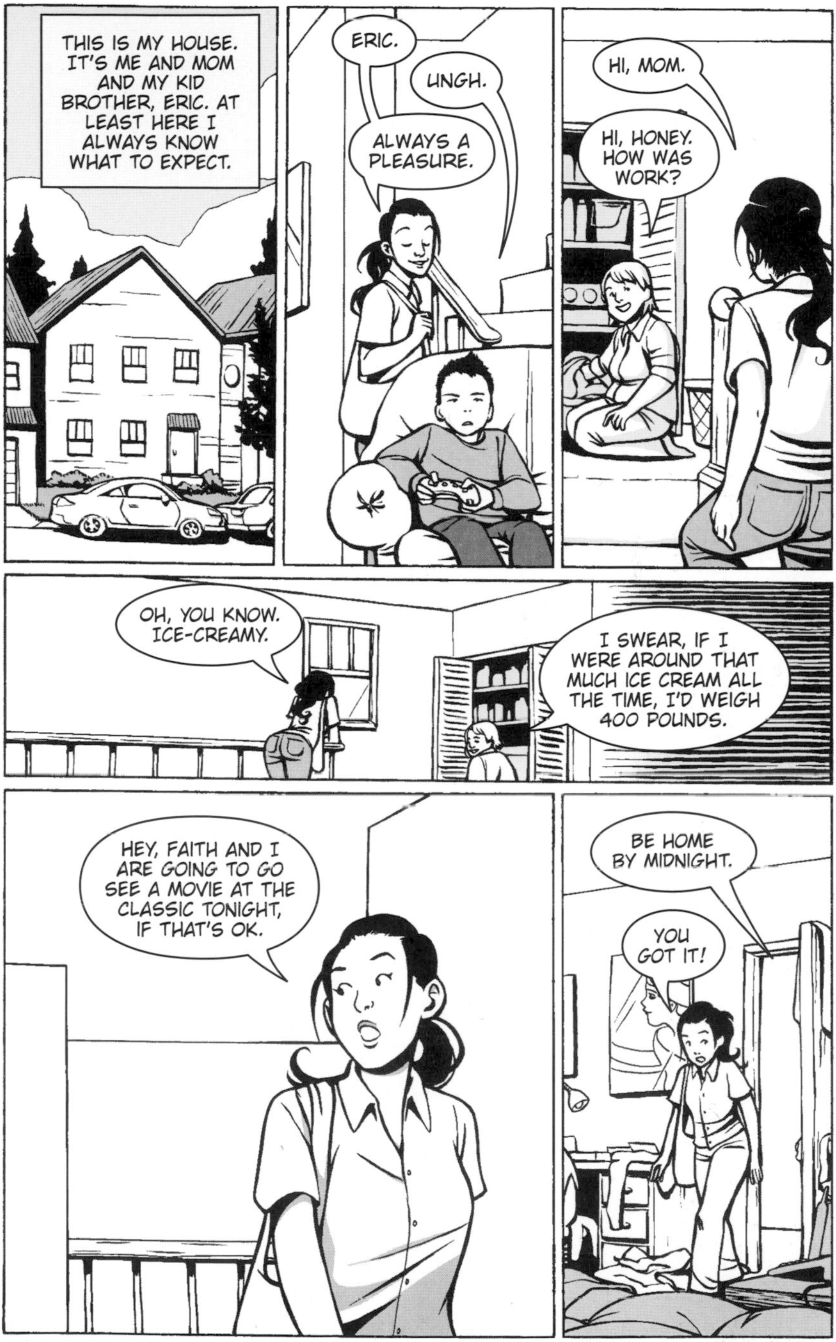
THIS IS MY HOUSE. IT'S ME AND MOM AND MY KID BROTHER, ERIC. AT LEAST HERE I ALWAYS KNOW WHAT TO EXPECT.
ERIC.
UNGH.
ALWAYS A PLEASURE.
HI, MOM.
HI, HONEY. HOW WAS WORK?
OH, YOU KNOW. ICE-CREAMY.
I SWEAR, IF I WERE AROUND THAT MUCH ICE CREAM ALL THE TIME, I'D WEIGH 400 POUNDS.
HEY, FAITH AND I ARE GOING TO GO SEE A MOVIE AT THE CLASSIC TONIGHT, IF THAT'S OK.
BE HOME BY MIDNIGHT.
YOU GOT IT!

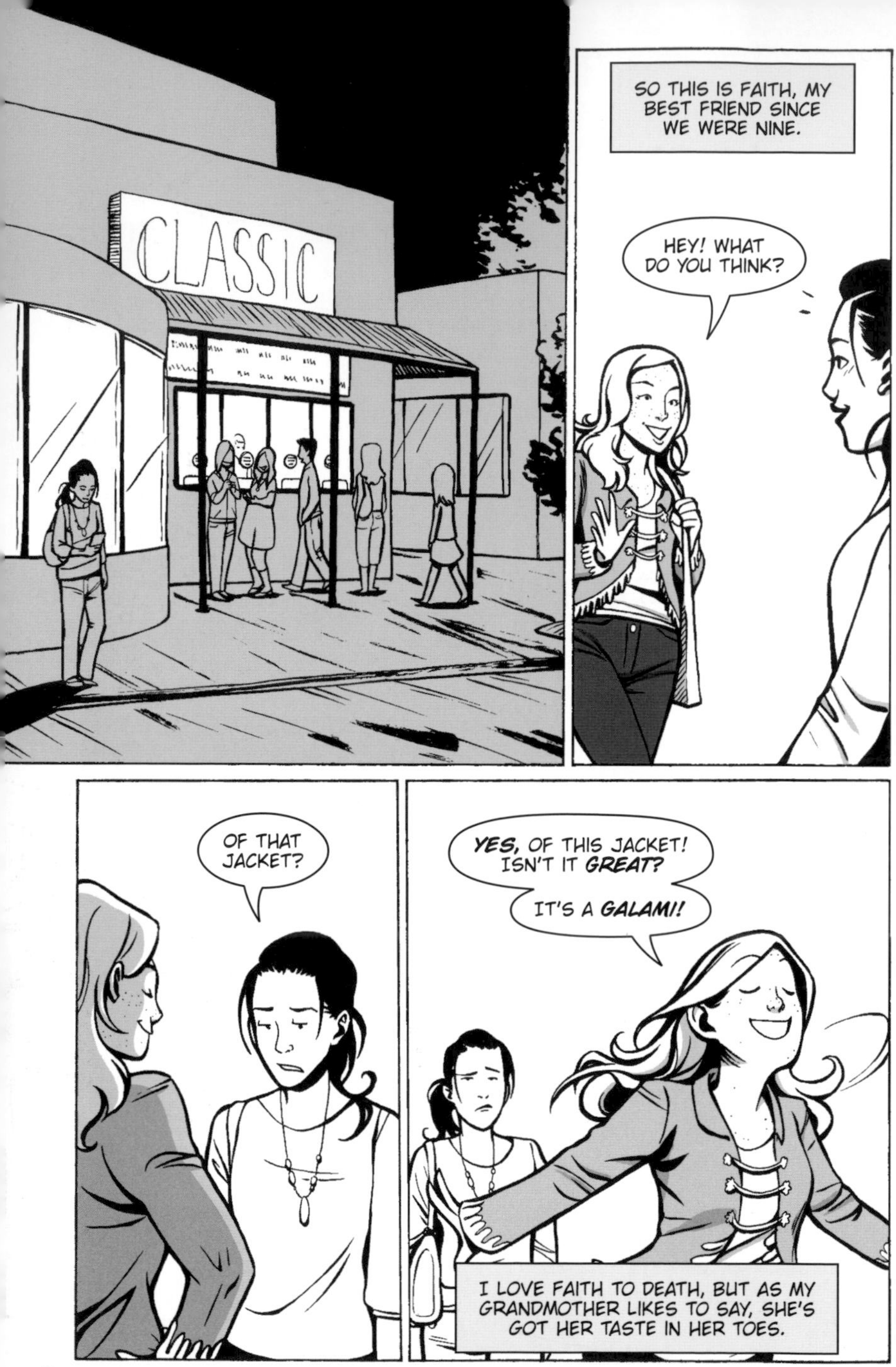
CLASSIC
SO THIS IS FAITH, MY BEST FRIEND SINCE WE WERE NINE.
HEY! WHAT DO YOU THINK?
OF THAT JACKET?
YES, OF THIS JACKET! ISN'T IT ***GREAT?***
IT'S A ***GALAMI!***
I LOVE FAITH TO DEATH, BUT AS MY GRANDMOTHER LIKES TO SAY, SHE'S GOT HER TASTE IN HER TOES.

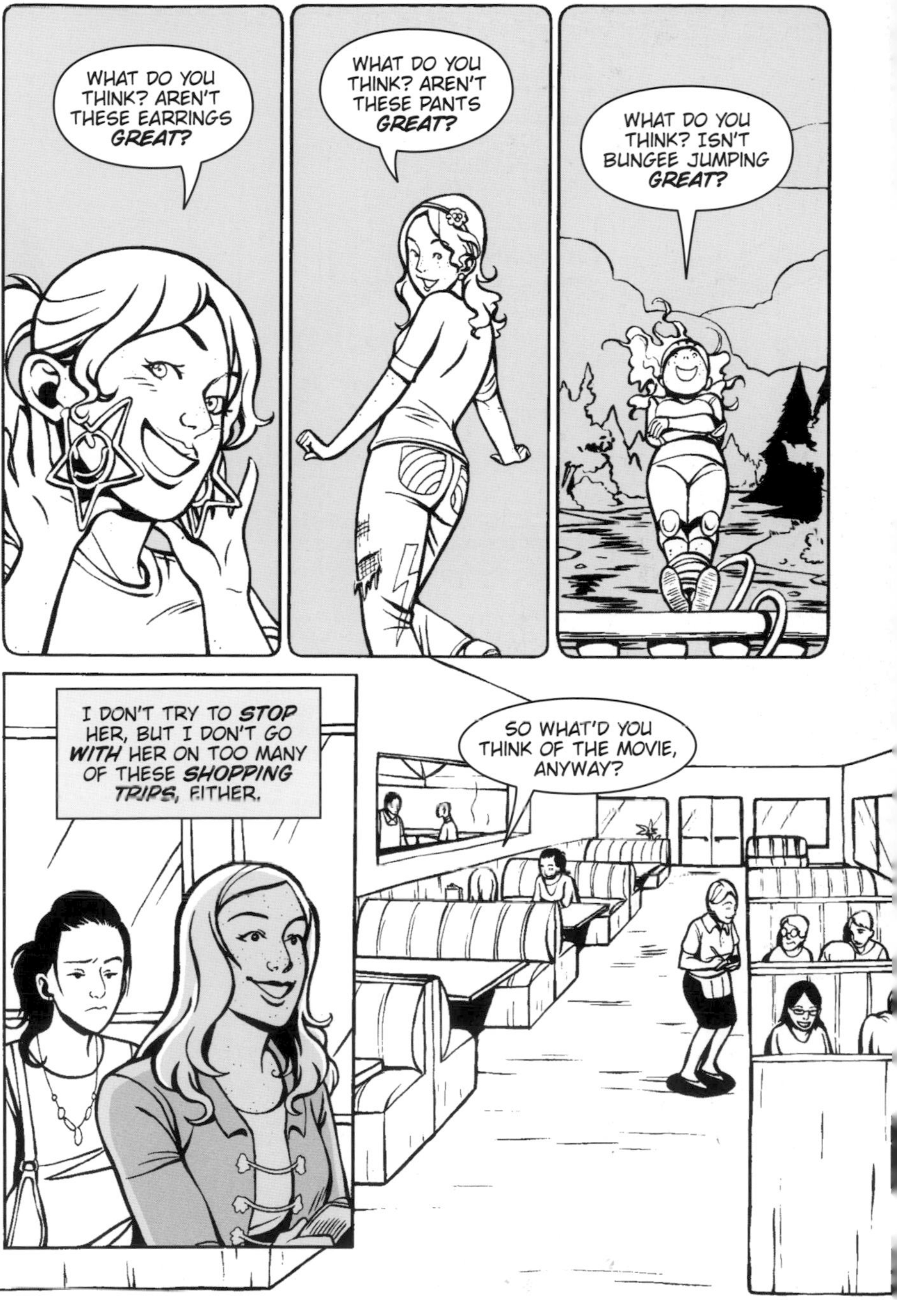

WHAT DO YOU THINK? AREN'T THESE EARRINGS **GREAT?**
WHAT DO YOU THINK? AREN'T THESE PANTS **GREAT?**
WHAT DO YOU THINK? ISN'T BUNGEE JUMPING **GREAT?**
I DON'T TRY TO **STOP** HER, BUT I DON'T GO **WITH** HER ON TOO MANY OF THESE **SHOPPING TRIPS**, EITHER.
SO WHAT'D YOU THINK OF THE MOVIE, ANYWAY?

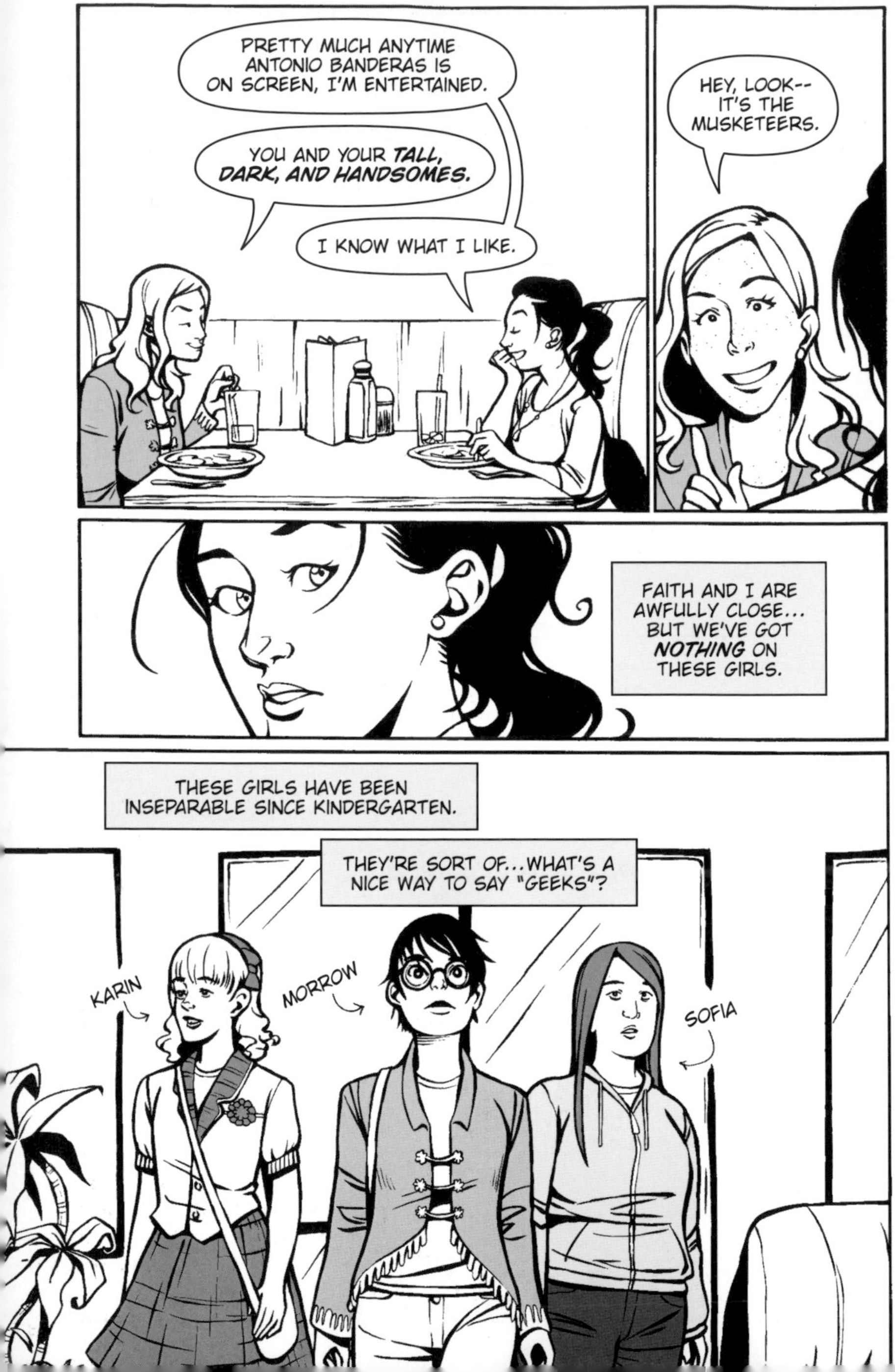
PRETTY MUCH ANYTIME ANTONIO BANDERAS IS ON SCREEN, I'M ENTERTAINED.
YOU AND YOUR TALL, DARK, AND HANDSOMES.
I KNOW WHAT I LIKE.
HEY, LOOK-- IT'S THE MUSKETEERS.
FAITH AND I ARE AWFULLY CLOSE... BUT WE'VE GOT NOTHING ON THESE GIRLS.
THESE GIRLS HAVE BEEN INSEPARABLE SINCE KINDERGARTEN.
THEY'RE SORT OF...WHAT'S A NICE WAY TO SAY "GEEKS"?
KARIN
MORROW
SOFIA

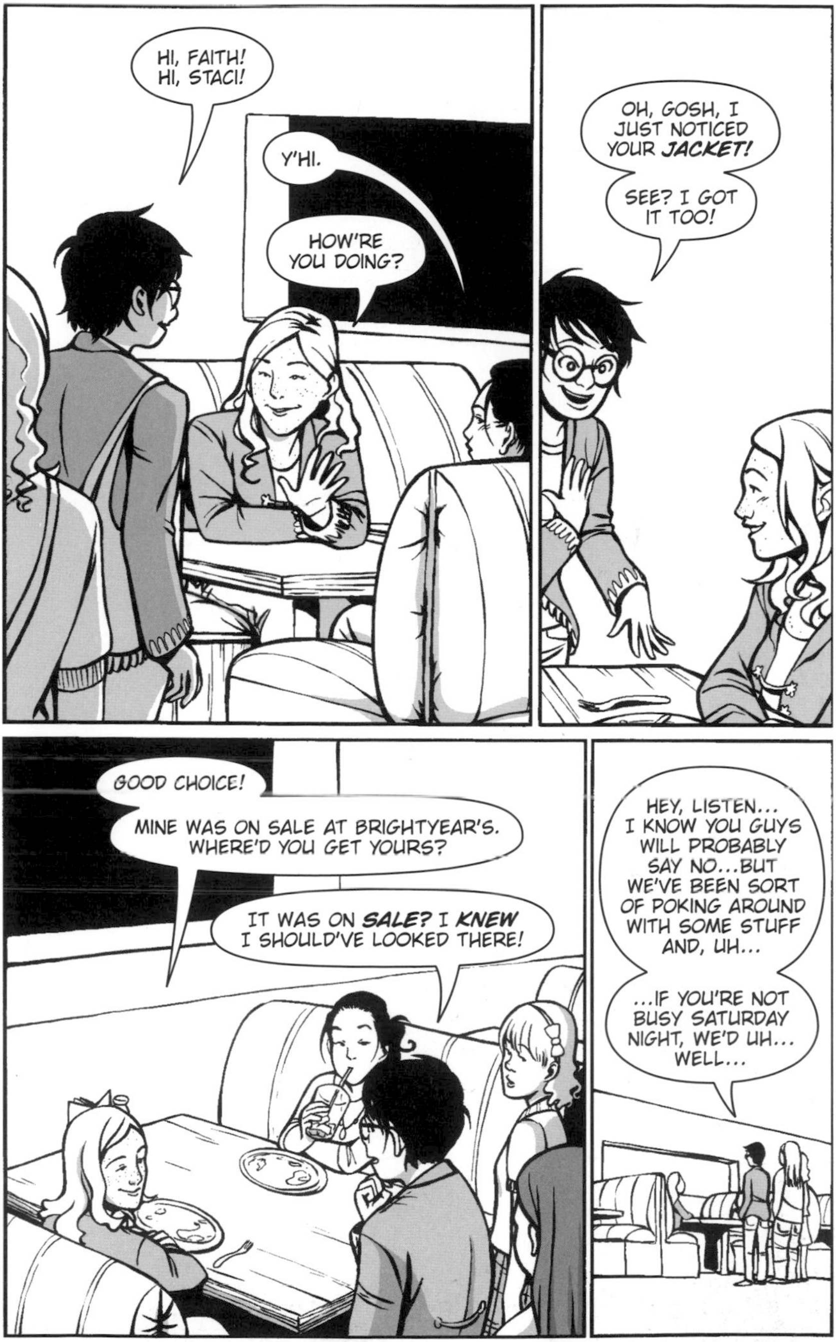
HI, FAITH! HI, STACI!
Y'HI.
HOW'RE YOU DOING?
OH, GOSH, I JUST NOTICED YOUR ***JACKET!***
SEE? I GOT IT TOO!
GOOD CHOICE!
MINE WAS ON SALE AT BRIGHTYEAR'S. WHERE'D YOU GET YOURS?
IT WAS ON ***SALE?*** I ***KNEW*** I SHOULD'VE LOOKED THERE!
HEY, LISTEN... I KNOW YOU GUYS WILL PROBABLY SAY NO...BUT WE'VE BEEN SORT OF POKING AROUND WITH SOME STUFF AND, UH...
...IF YOU'RE NOT BUSY SATURDAY NIGHT, WE'D UH... WELL...

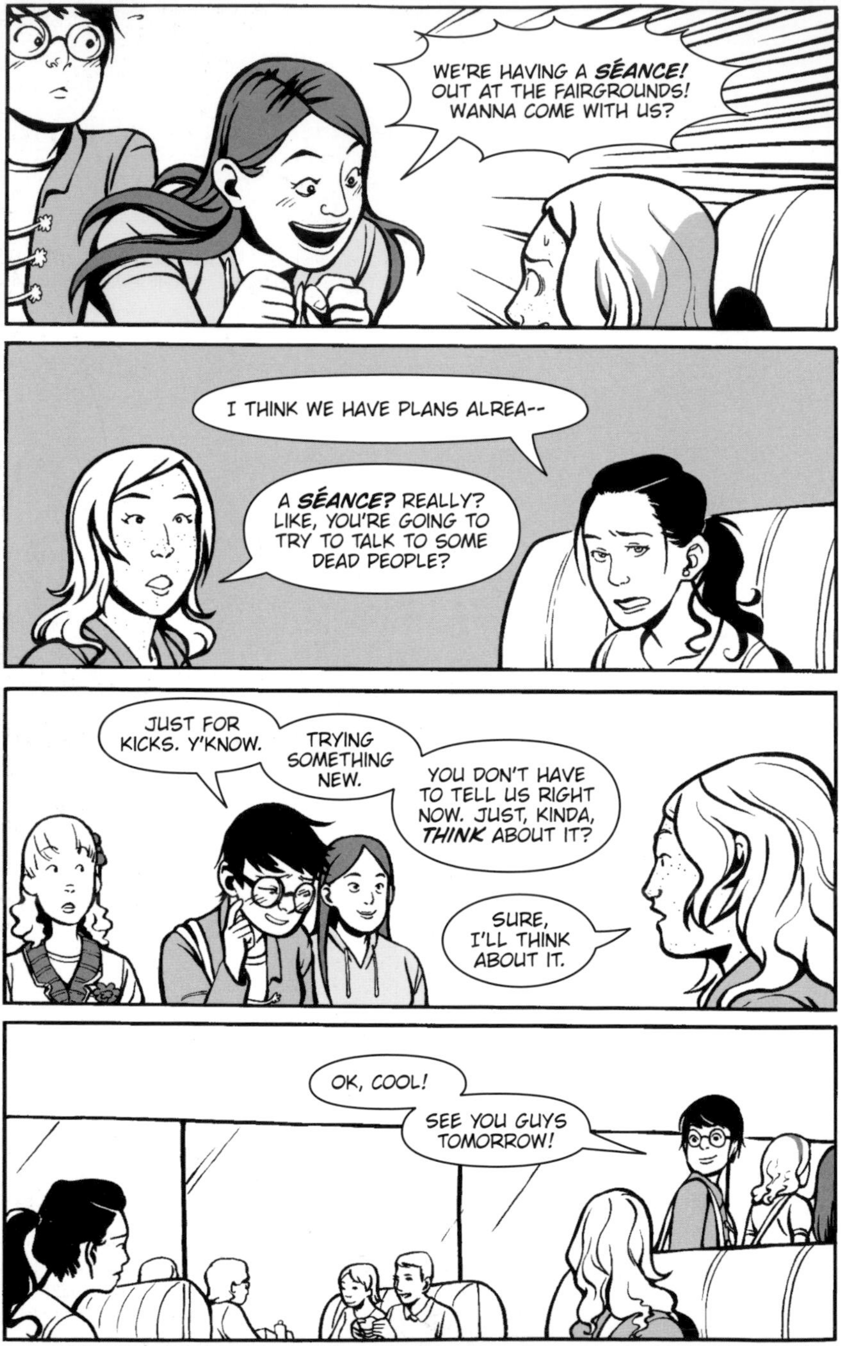

WE'RE HAVING A ***SÉANCE!*** OUT AT THE FAIRGROUNDS! WANNA COME WITH US?
I THINK WE HAVE PLANS ALREA--
A ***SÉANCE?*** REALLY? LIKE, YOU'RE GOING TO TRY TO TALK TO SOME DEAD PEOPLE?
JUST FOR KICKS. Y'KNOW.
TRYING SOMETHING NEW.
YOU DON'T HAVE TO TELL US RIGHT NOW. JUST, KINDA, ***THINK*** ABOUT IT?
SURE, I'LL THINK ABOUT IT.
OK, COOL!
SEE YOU GUYS TOMORROW!

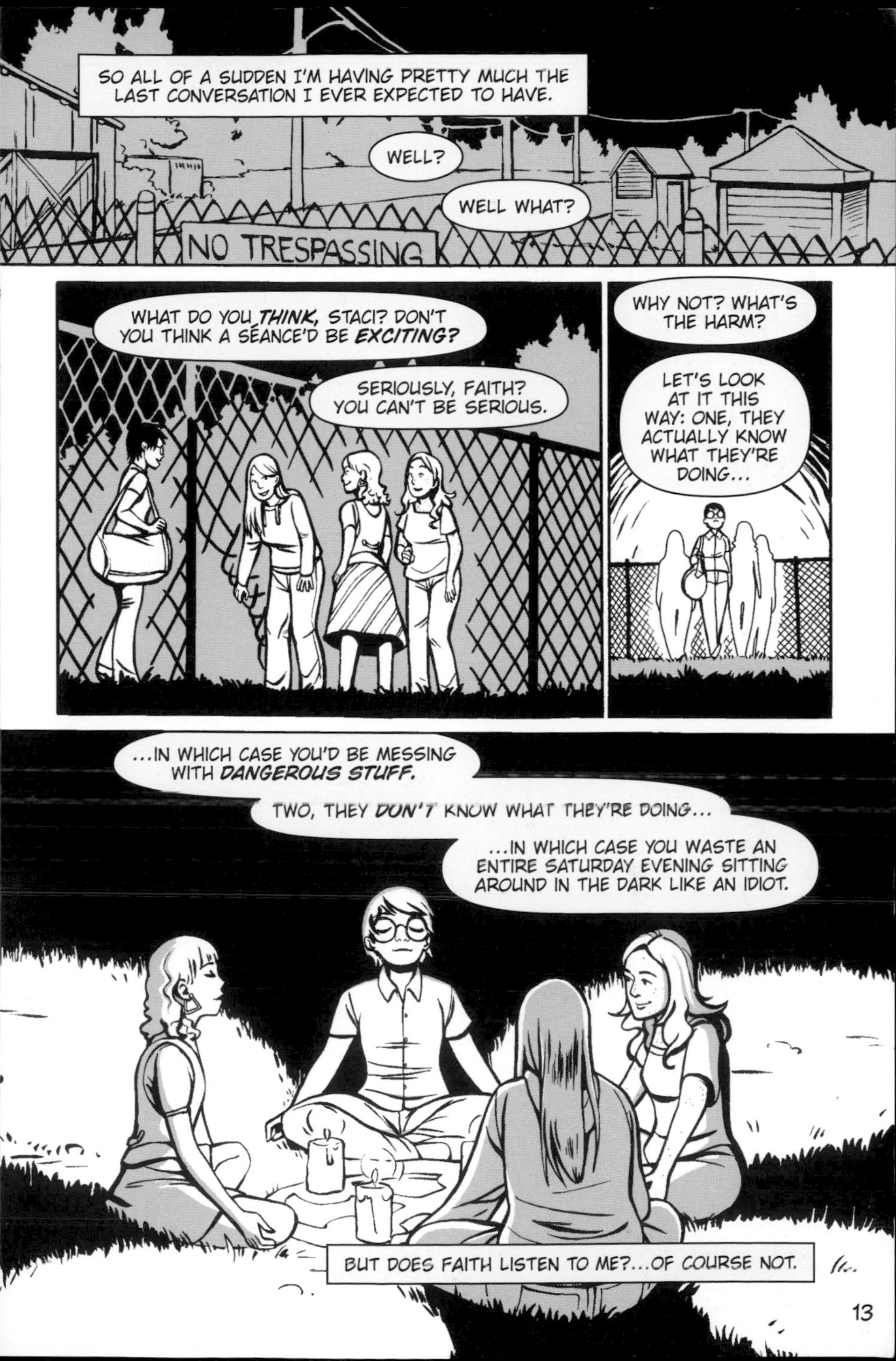
SO ALL OF A SUDDEN I'M HAVING PRETTY MUCH THE LAST CONVERSATION I EVER EXPECTED TO HAVE.
WELL?
WELL WHAT?
NO TRESPASSING
WHAT DO YOU *THINK*, STACI? DON'T YOU THINK A SÉANCE'D BE *EXCITING?*
SERIOUSLY, FAITH? YOU CAN'T BE SERIOUS.
WHY NOT? WHAT'S THE HARM?
LET'S LOOK AT IT THIS WAY: ONE, THEY ACTUALLY KNOW WHAT THEY'RE DOING...
...IN WHICH CASE YOU'D BE MESSING WITH *DANGEROUS STUFF.*
TWO, THEY *DON'T* KNOW WHAT THEY'RE DOING...
...IN WHICH CASE YOU WASTE AN ENTIRE SATURDAY EVENING SITTING AROUND IN THE DARK LIKE AN IDIOT.
BUT DOES FAITH LISTEN TO ME?...OF COURSE NOT.

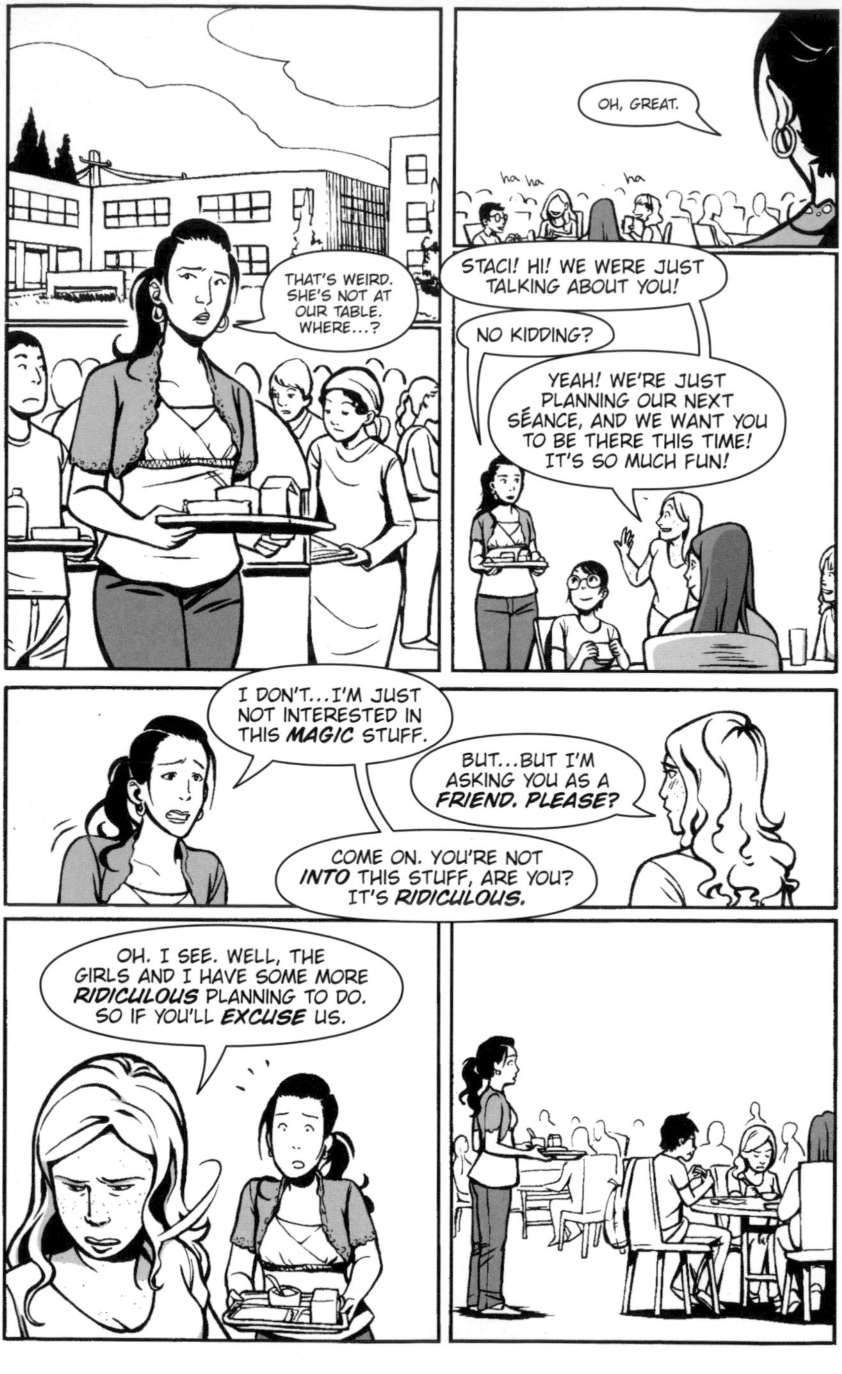
THAT'S WEIRD. SHE'S NOT AT OUR TABLE. WHERE...?
OH, GREAT.
ha ha
ha
STACI! HI! WE WERE JUST TALKING ABOUT YOU!
NO KIDDING?
YEAH! WE'RE JUST PLANNING OUR NEXT SÉANCE, AND WE WANT YOU TO BE THERE THIS TIME! IT'S SO MUCH FUN!
I DON'T...I'M JUST NOT INTERESTED IN THIS *MAGIC* STUFF.
BUT...BUT I'M ASKING YOU AS A *FRIEND. PLEASE?*
COME ON. YOU'RE NOT *INTO* THIS STUFF, ARE YOU? IT'S *RIDICULOUS.*
OH. I SEE. WELL, THE GIRLS AND I HAVE SOME MORE *RIDICULOUS* PLANNING TO DO. SO IF YOU'LL *EXCUSE* US.

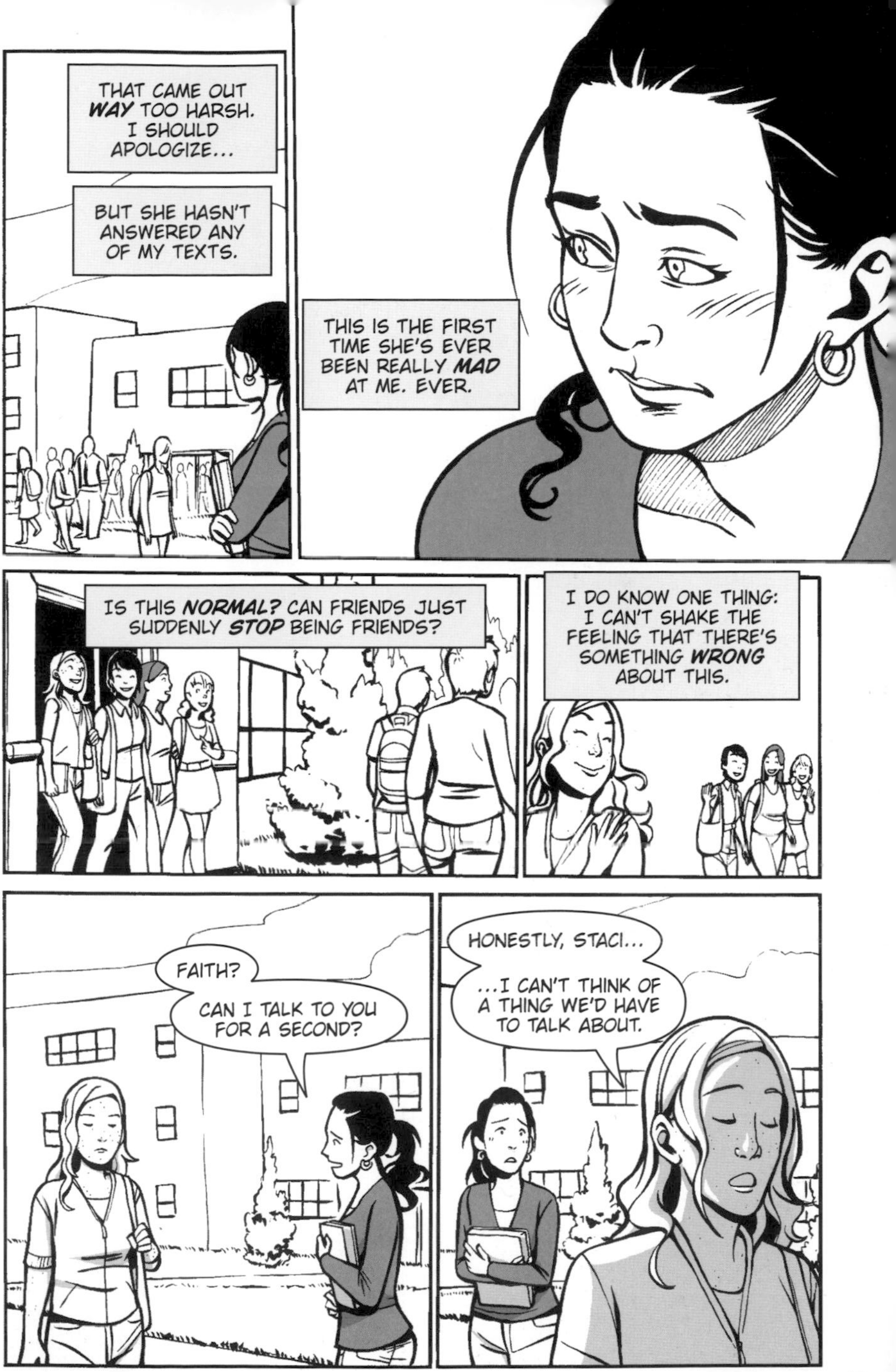

THAT CAME OUT WAY TOO HARSH. I SHOULD APOLOGIZE...
BUT SHE HASN'T ANSWERED ANY OF MY TEXTS.
THIS IS THE FIRST TIME SHE'S EVER BEEN REALLY MAD AT ME. EVER.
IS THIS NORMAL? CAN FRIENDS JUST SUDDENLY STOP BEING FRIENDS?
I DO KNOW ONE THING: I CAN'T SHAKE THE FEELING THAT THERE'S SOMETHING WRONG ABOUT THIS.
FAITH?
CAN I TALK TO YOU FOR A SECOND?
HONESTLY, STACI...
...I CAN'T THINK OF A THING WE'D HAVE TO TALK ABOUT.

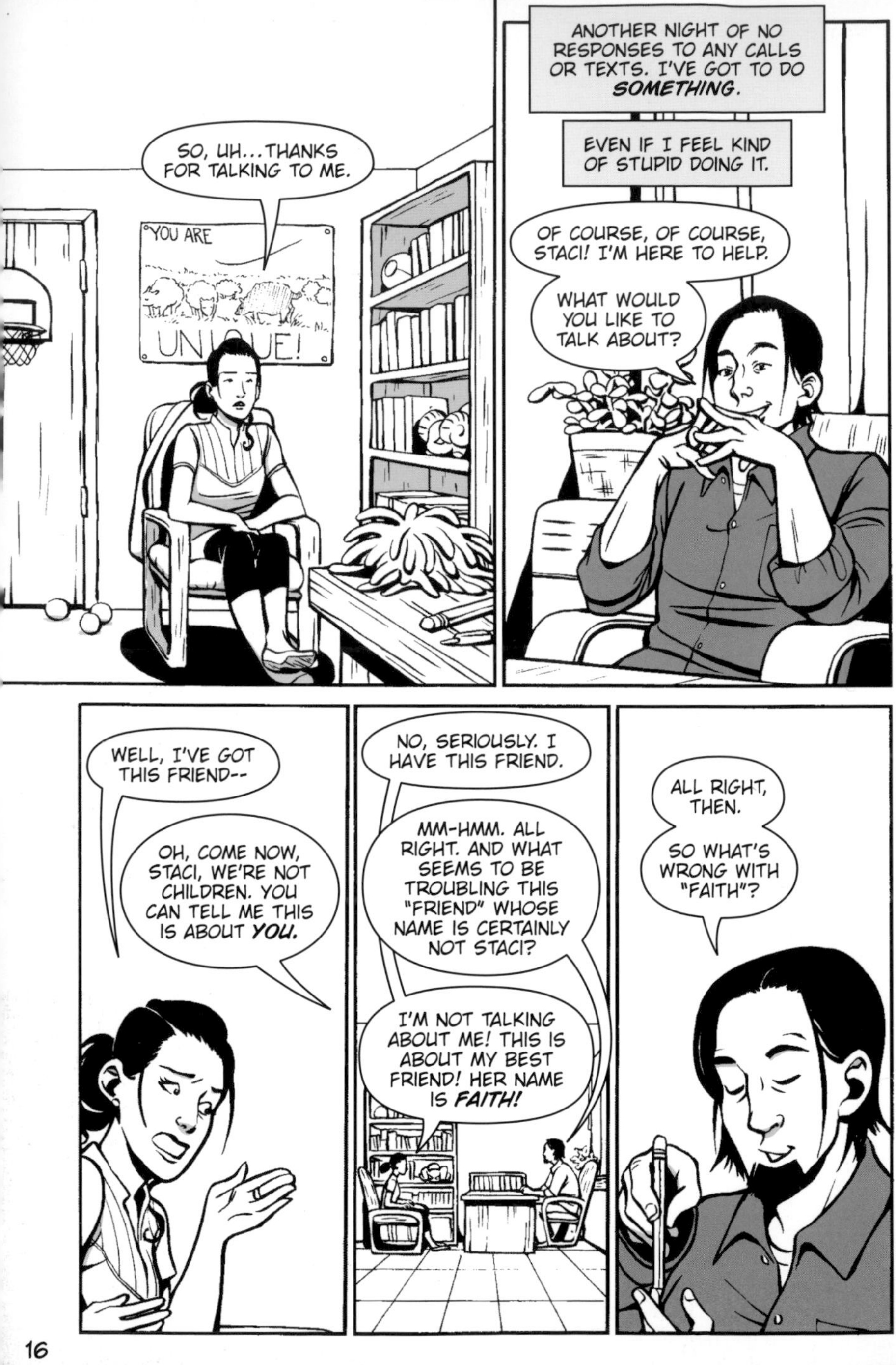
SO, UH...THANKS FOR TALKING TO ME.
YOU ARE UNIQUE!
ANOTHER NIGHT OF NO RESPONSES TO ANY CALLS OR TEXTS. I'VE GOT TO DO SOMETHING.
EVEN IF I FEEL KIND OF STUPID DOING IT.
OF COURSE, OF COURSE, STACI! I'M HERE TO HELP.
WHAT WOULD YOU LIKE TO TALK ABOUT?
WELL, I'VE GOT THIS FRIEND--
OH, COME NOW, STACI, WE'RE NOT CHILDREN. YOU CAN TELL ME THIS IS ABOUT YOU.
NO, SERIOUSLY. I HAVE THIS FRIEND.
MM-HMM. ALL RIGHT. AND WHAT SEEMS TO BE TROUBLING THIS "FRIEND" WHOSE NAME IS CERTAINLY NOT STACI?
I'M NOT TALKING ABOUT ME! THIS IS ABOUT MY BEST FRIEND! HER NAME IS FAITH!
ALL RIGHT, THEN.
SO WHAT'S WRONG WITH "FAITH"?

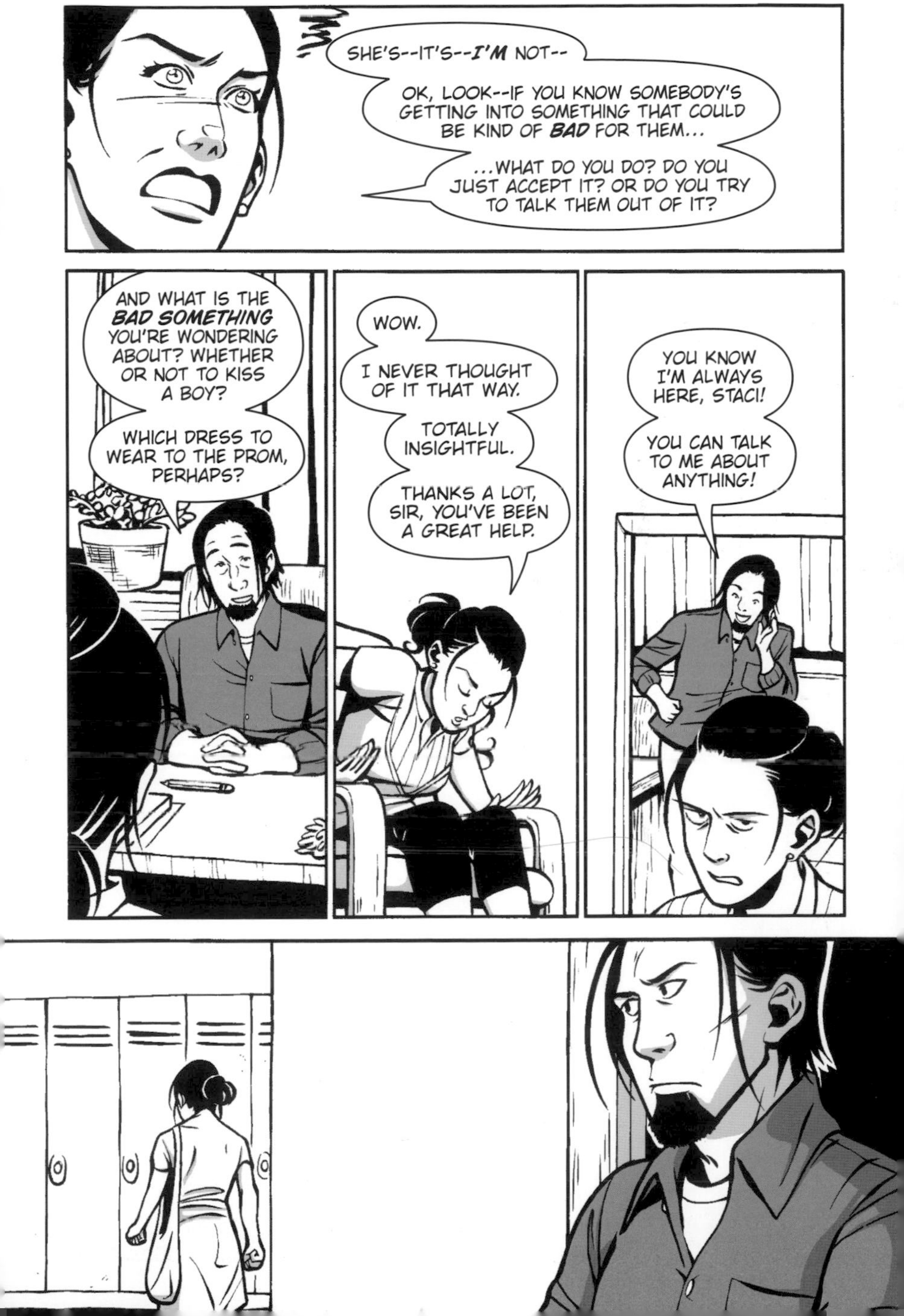
SHE'S--IT'S--*I'M* NOT--
OK, LOOK--IF YOU KNOW SOMEBODY'S GETTING INTO SOMETHING THAT COULD BE KIND OF *BAD* FOR THEM...
...WHAT DO YOU DO? DO YOU JUST ACCEPT IT? OR DO YOU TRY TO TALK THEM OUT OF IT?
AND WHAT IS THE *BAD SOMETHING* YOU'RE WONDERING ABOUT? WHETHER OR NOT TO KISS A BOY?
WHICH DRESS TO WEAR TO THE PROM, PERHAPS?
WOW.
I NEVER THOUGHT OF IT THAT WAY.
TOTALLY INSIGHTFUL.
THANKS A LOT, SIR, YOU'VE BEEN A GREAT HELP.
YOU KNOW I'M ALWAYS HERE, STACI!
YOU CAN TALK TO ME ABOUT ANYTHING!

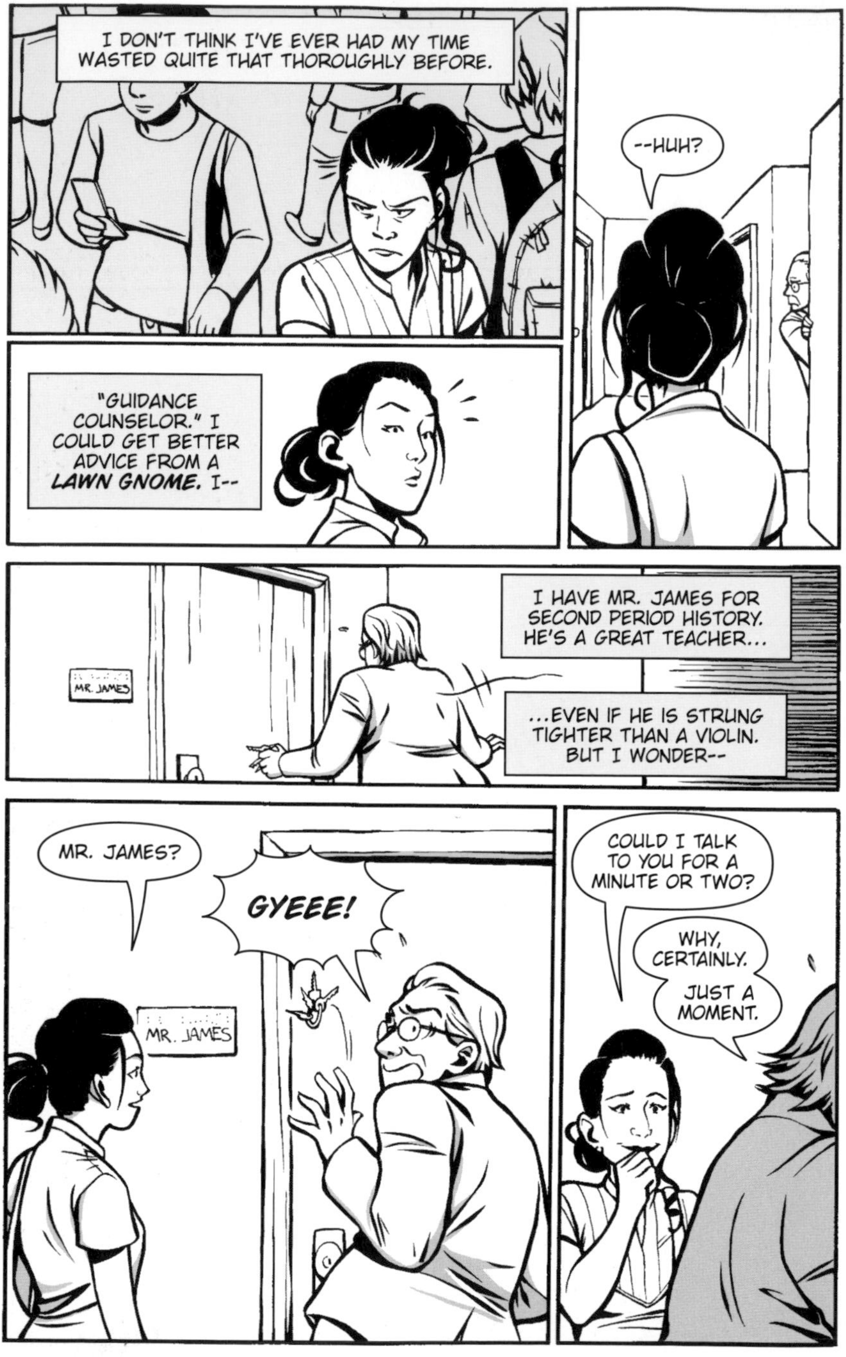
I DON'T THINK I'VE EVER HAD MY TIME WASTED QUITE THAT THOROUGHLY BEFORE.
"GUIDANCE COUNSELOR." I COULD GET BETTER ADVICE FROM A LAWN GNOME. I--
--HUH?
MR. JAMES
I HAVE MR. JAMES FOR SECOND PERIOD HISTORY. HE'S A GREAT TEACHER...
...EVEN IF HE IS STRUNG TIGHTER THAN A VIOLIN. BUT I WONDER--
MR. JAMES?
GYEEE!
MR. JAMES
COULD I TALK TO YOU FOR A MINUTE OR TWO?
WHY, CERTAINLY.
JUST A MOMENT.

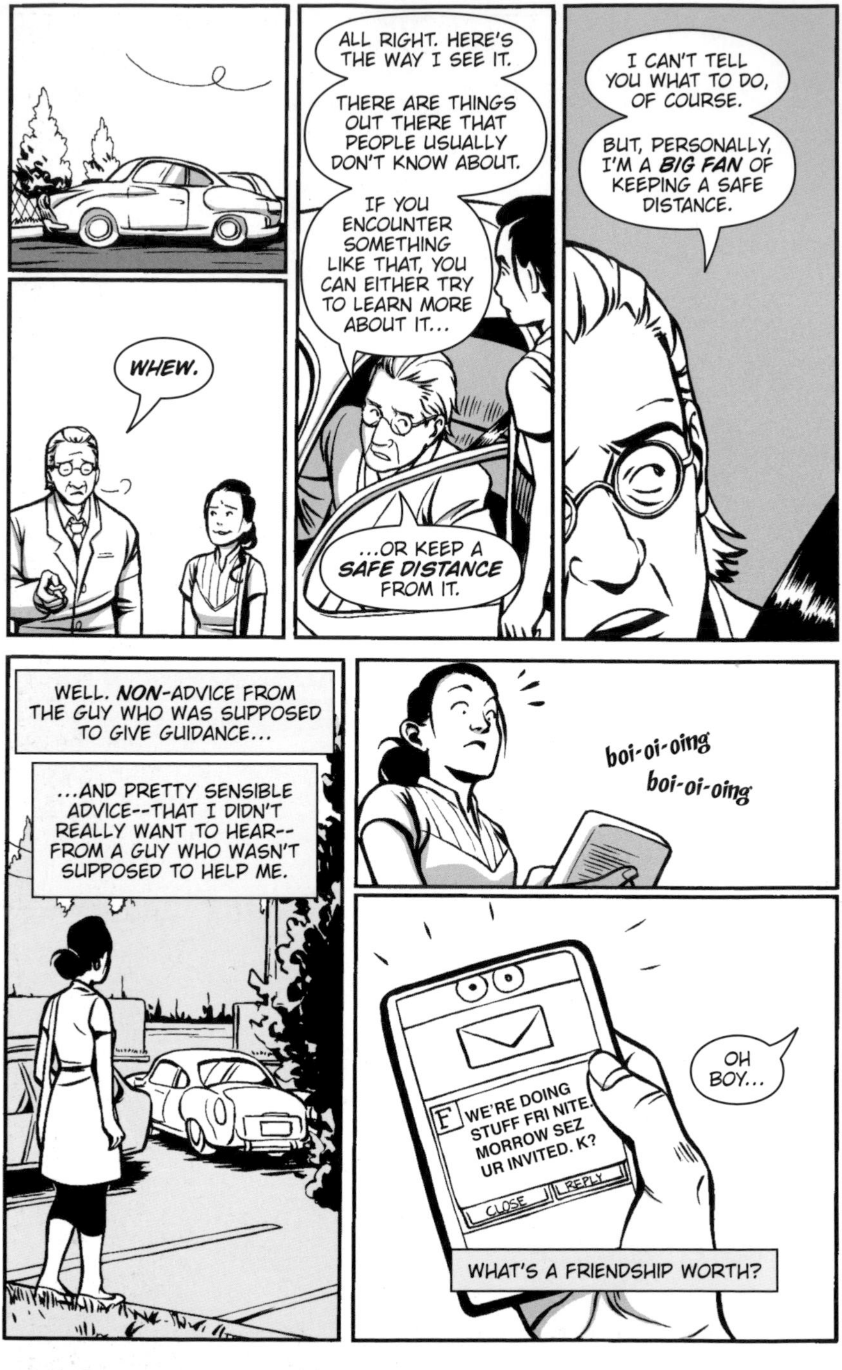
WHEW.
ALL RIGHT. HERE'S THE WAY I SEE IT.
THERE ARE THINGS OUT THERE THAT PEOPLE USUALLY DON'T KNOW ABOUT.
IF YOU ENCOUNTER SOMETHING LIKE THAT, YOU CAN EITHER TRY TO LEARN MORE ABOUT IT...
...OR KEEP A SAFE DISTANCE FROM IT.
I CAN'T TELL YOU WHAT TO DO, OF COURSE.
BUT, PERSONALLY, I'M A BIG FAN OF KEEPING A SAFE DISTANCE.
WELL. NON-ADVICE FROM THE GUY WHO WAS SUPPOSED TO GIVE GUIDANCE...
...AND PRETTY SENSIBLE ADVICE--THAT I DIDN'T REALLY WANT TO HEAR--FROM A GUY WHO WASN'T SUPPOSED TO HELP ME.
boi-oi-oing
boi-oi-oing
F
WE'RE DOING STUFF FRI NITE. MORROW SEZ UR INVITED. K?
CLOSE
REPLY
OH BOY...
WHAT'S A FRIENDSHIP WORTH?

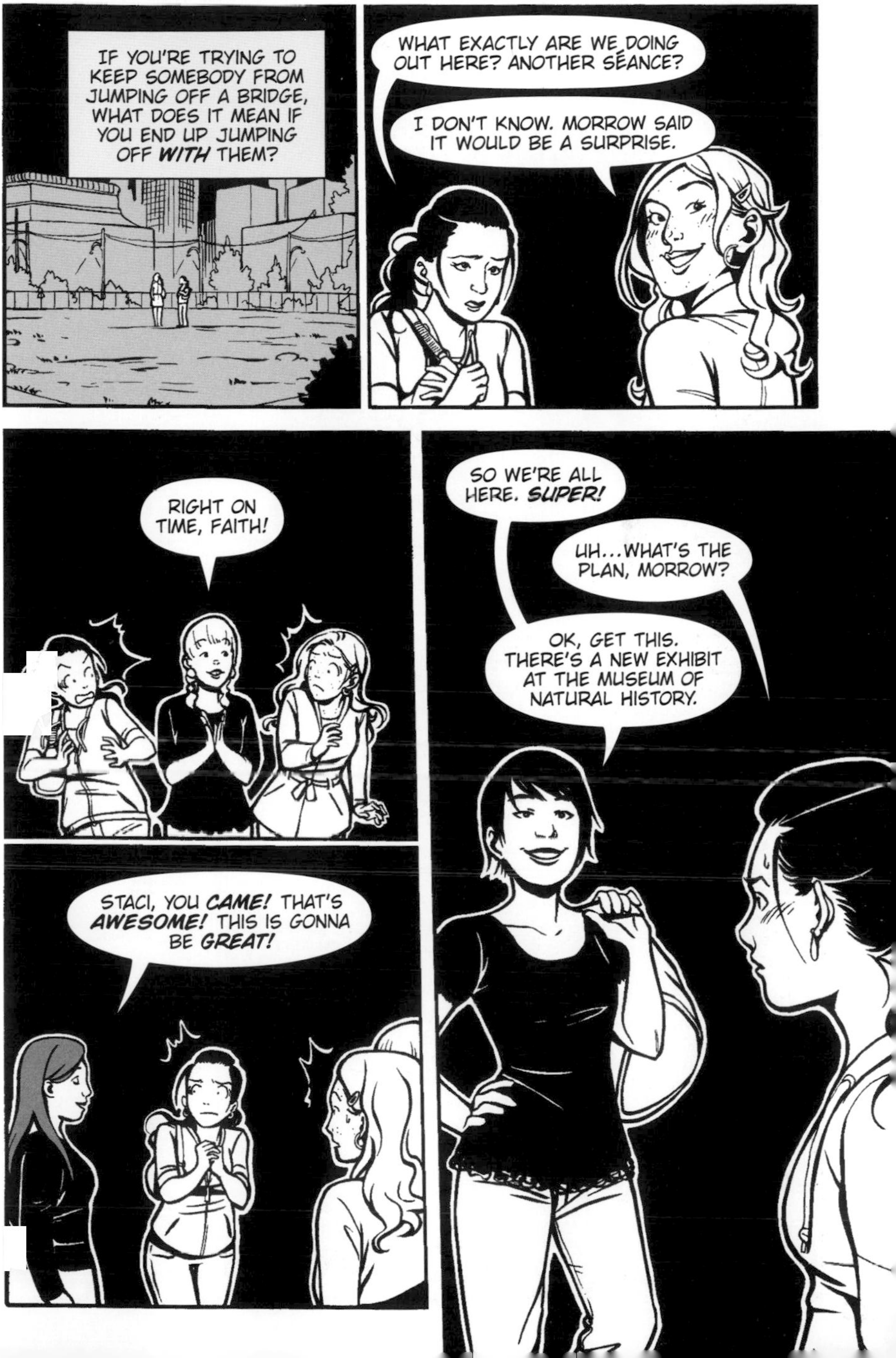
IF YOU'RE TRYING TO KEEP SOMEBODY FROM JUMPING OFF A BRIDGE, WHAT DOES IT MEAN IF YOU END UP JUMPING OFF WITH THEM?
WHAT EXACTLY ARE WE DOING OUT HERE? ANOTHER SÉANCE?
I DON'T KNOW. MORROW SAID IT WOULD BE A SURPRISE.
RIGHT ON TIME, FAITH!
STACI, YOU CAME! THAT'S AWESOME! THIS IS GONNA BE GREAT!
SO WE'RE ALL HERE. SUPER!
UH...WHAT'S THE PLAN, MORROW?
OK, GET THIS. THERE'S A NEW EXHIBIT AT THE MUSEUM OF NATURAL HISTORY.

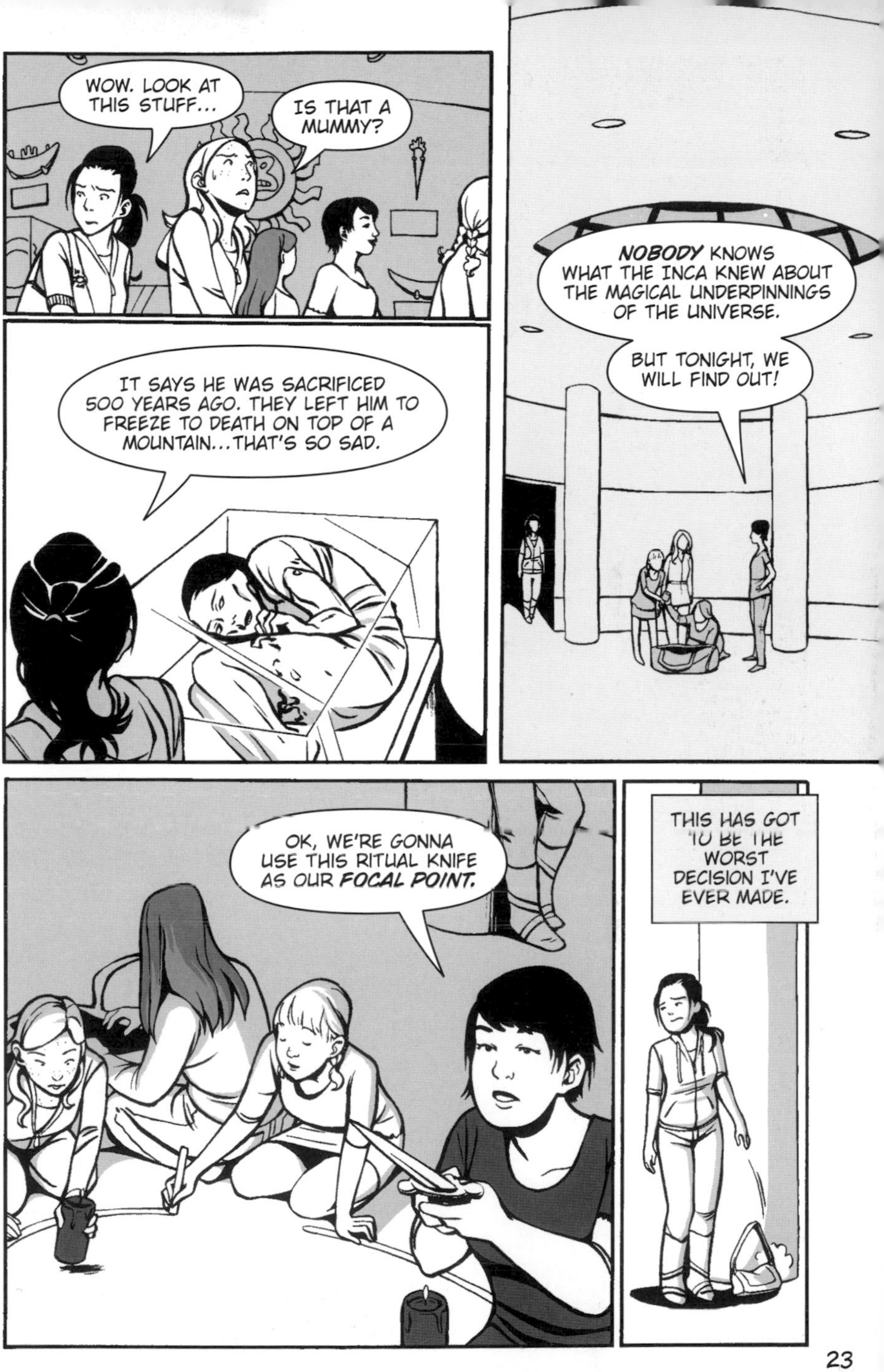

WOW. LOOK AT THIS STUFF...
IS THAT A MUMMY?
IT SAYS HE WAS SACRIFICED 500 YEARS AGO. THEY LEFT HIM TO FREEZE TO DEATH ON TOP OF A MOUNTAIN...THAT'S SO SAD.
NOBODY KNOWS WHAT THE INCA KNEW ABOUT THE MAGICAL UNDERPINNINGS OF THE UNIVERSE.
BUT TONIGHT, WE WILL FIND OUT!
OK, WE'RE GONNA USE THIS RITUAL KNIFE AS OUR FOCAL POINT.
THIS HAS GOT TO BE THE WORST DECISION I'VE EVER MADE.

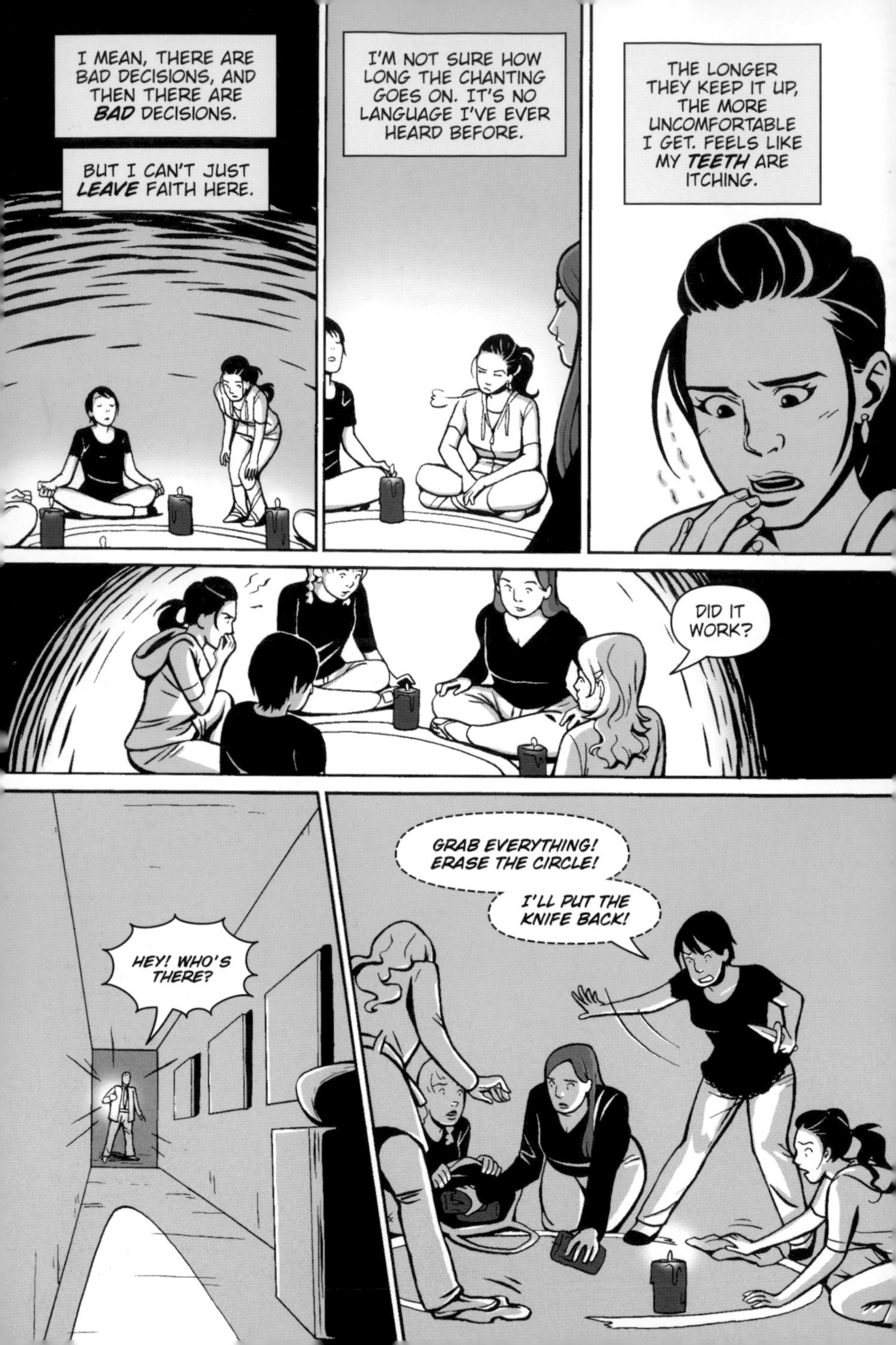
I MEAN, THERE ARE BAD DECISIONS, AND THEN THERE ARE *BAD* DECISIONS.
BUT I CAN'T JUST *LEAVE* FAITH HERE.
I'M NOT SURE HOW LONG THE CHANTING GOES ON. IT'S NO LANGUAGE I'VE EVER HEARD BEFORE.
THE LONGER THEY KEEP IT UP, THE MORE UNCOMFORTABLE I GET. FEELS LIKE MY *TEETH* ARE ITCHING.
DID IT WORK?
HEY! WHO'S THERE?
GRAB EVERYTHING! ERASE THE CIRCLE!
I'LL PUT THE KNIFE BACK!

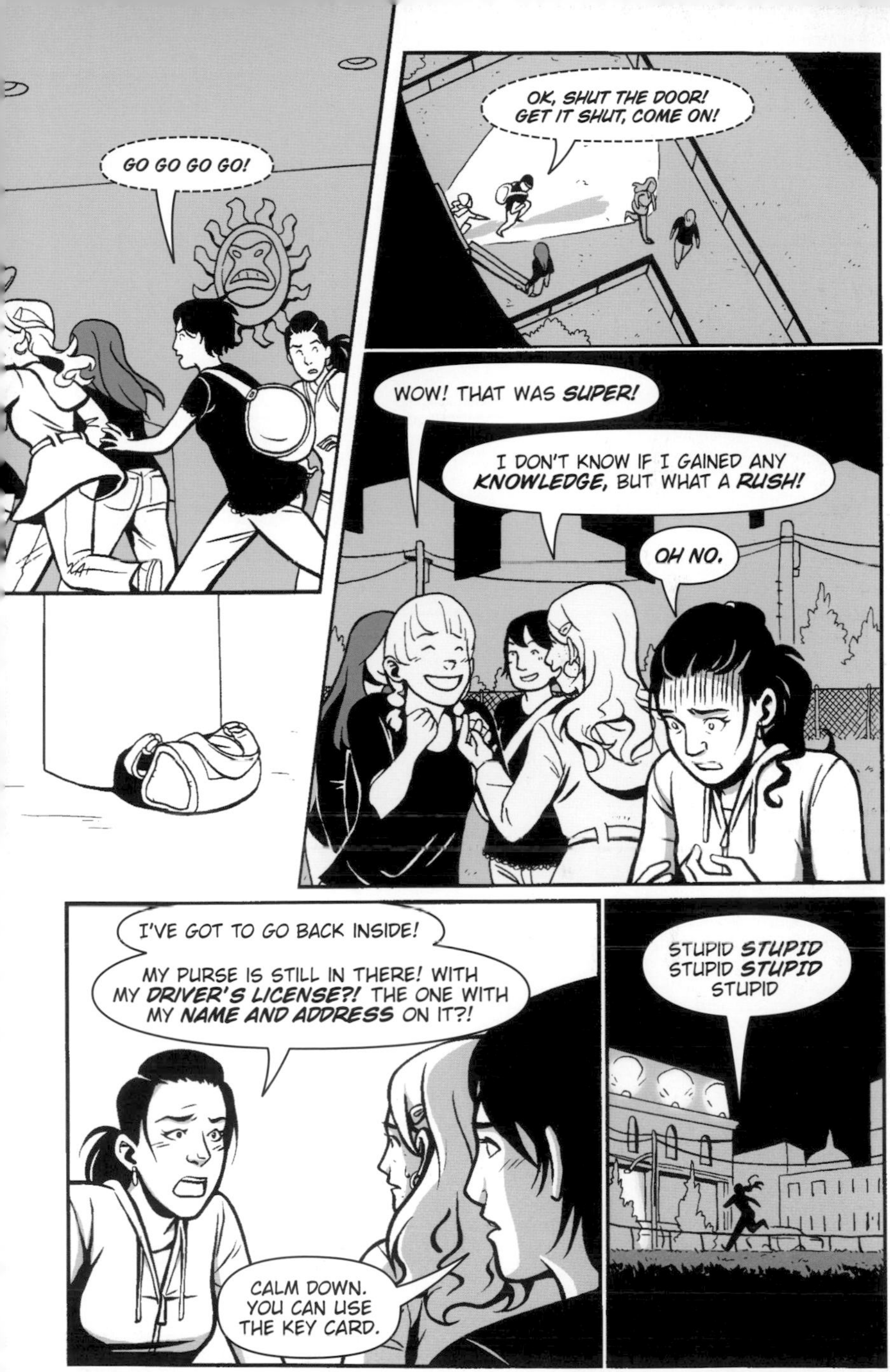
GO GO GO GO!
OK, SHUT THE DOOR! GET IT SHUT, COME ON!
WOW! THAT WAS SUPER!
I DON'T KNOW IF I GAINED ANY KNOWLEDGE, BUT WHAT A RUSH!
OH NO.
I'VE GOT TO GO BACK INSIDE!
MY PURSE IS STILL IN THERE! WITH MY DRIVER'S LICENSE?! THE ONE WITH MY NAME AND ADDRESS ON IT?!
CALM DOWN. YOU CAN USE THE KEY CARD.
STUPID STUPID STUPID STUPID STUPID

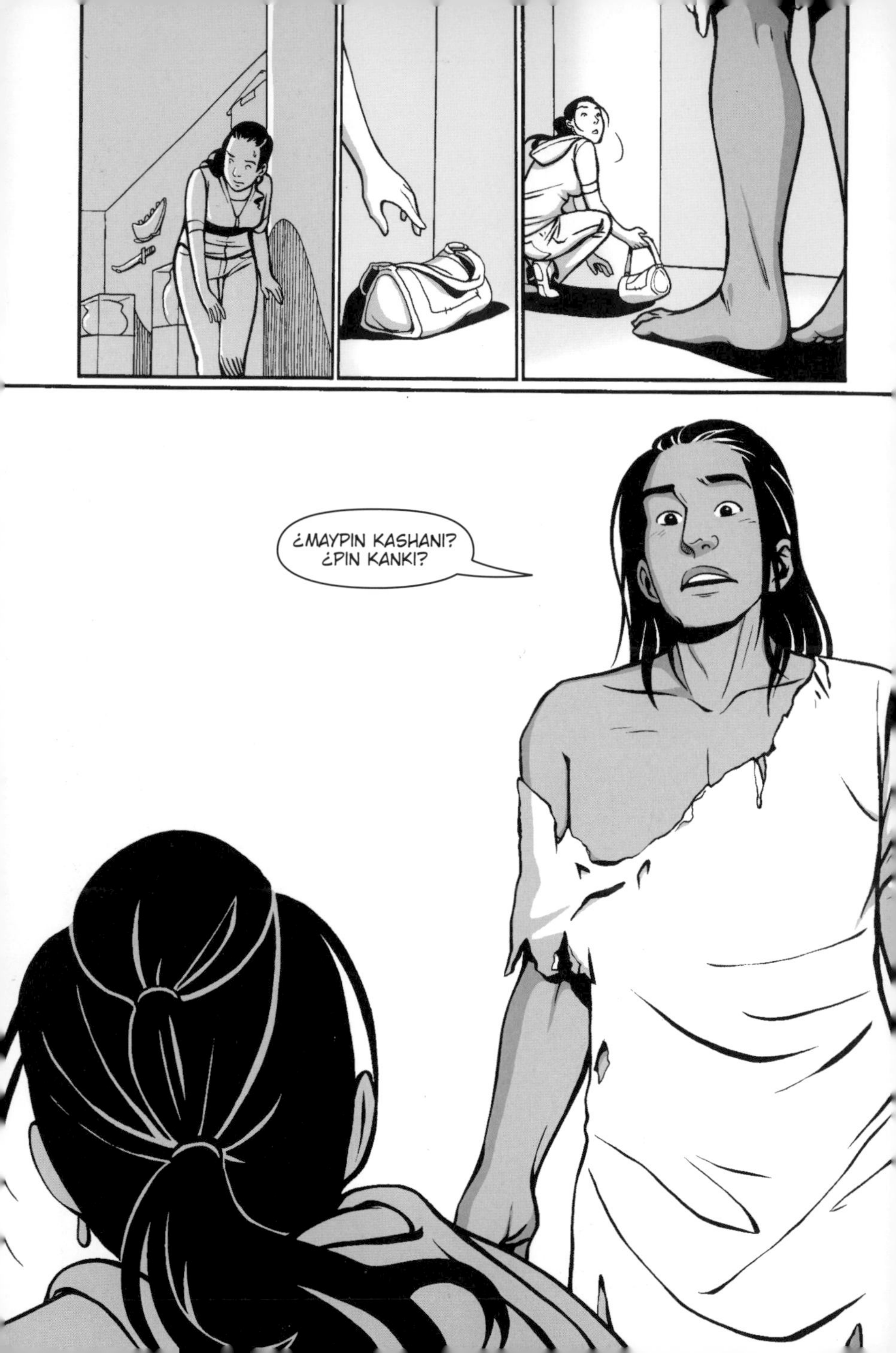
¿MAYPIN KASHANI? ¿PIN KANKI?

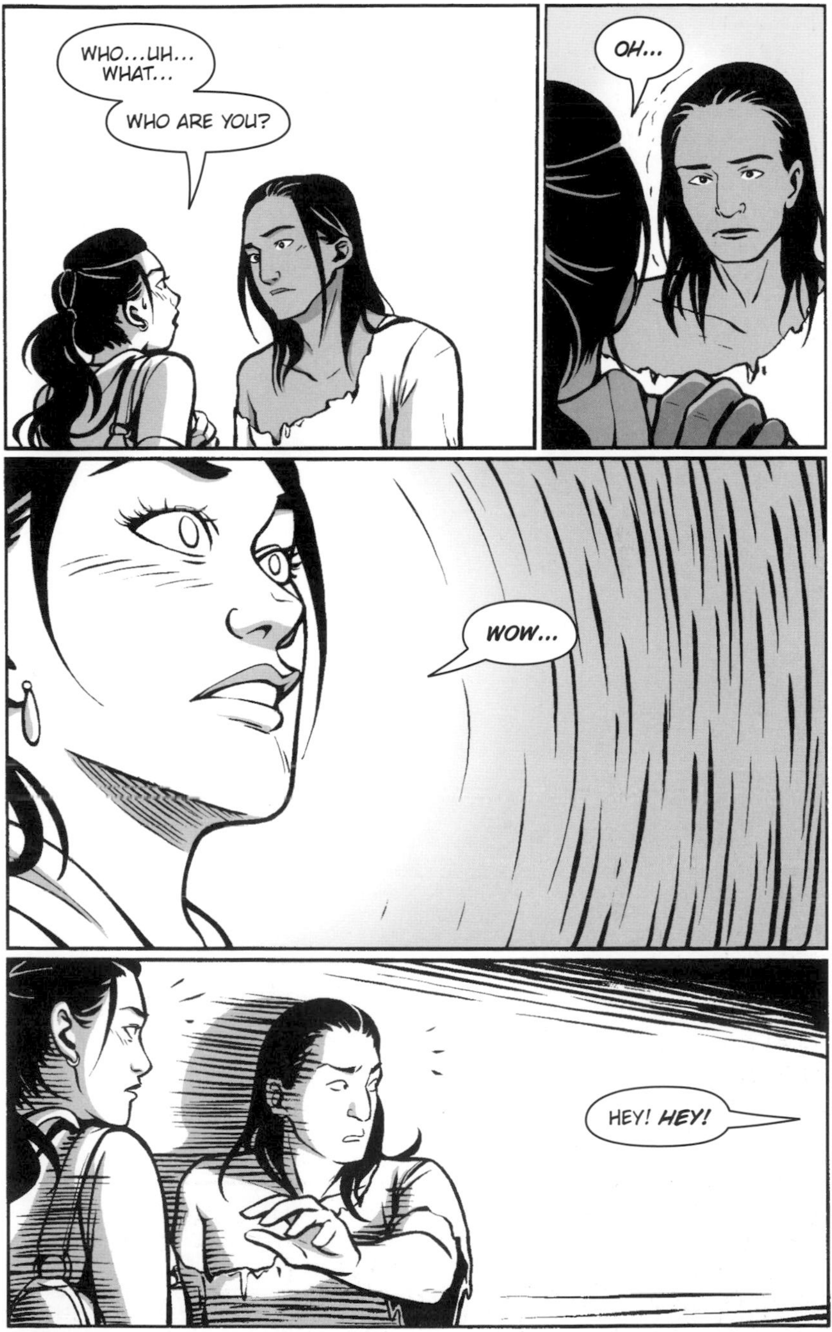
WHO...UH...
WHAT...
WHO ARE YOU?
OH...
WOW...
HEY! HEY!

CHAPTER TWO

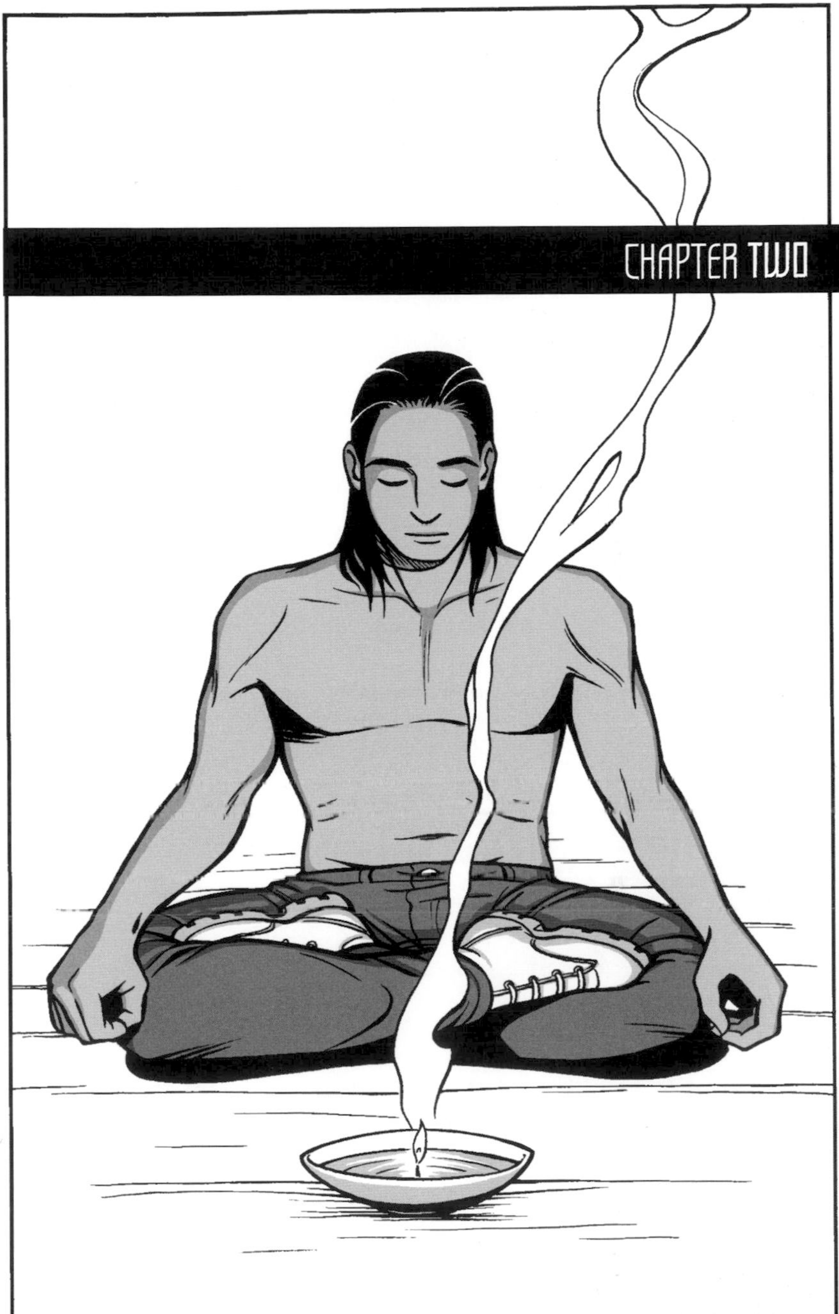

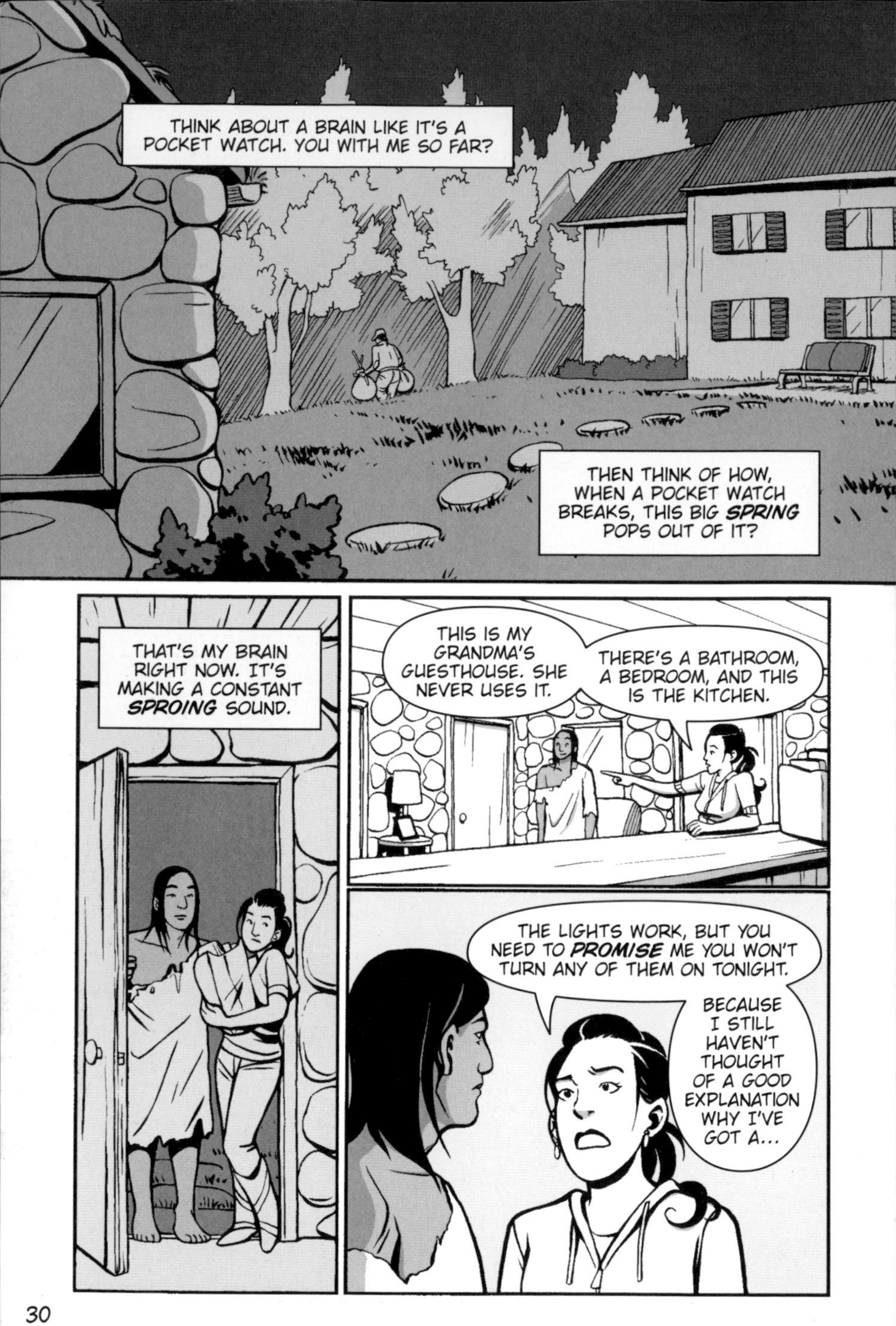
THINK ABOUT A BRAIN LIKE IT'S A POCKET WATCH. YOU WITH ME SO FAR?
THEN THINK OF HOW, WHEN A POCKET WATCH BREAKS, THIS BIG SPRING POPS OUT OF IT?
THAT'S MY BRAIN RIGHT NOW. IT'S MAKING A CONSTANT SPROING SOUND.
THIS IS MY GRANDMA'S GUESTHOUSE. SHE NEVER USES IT.
THERE'S A BATHROOM, A BEDROOM, AND THIS IS THE KITCHEN.
THE LIGHTS WORK, BUT YOU NEED TO PROMISE ME YOU WON'T TURN ANY OF THEM ON TONIGHT.
BECAUSE I STILL HAVEN'T THOUGHT OF A GOOD EXPLANATION WHY I'VE GOT A...

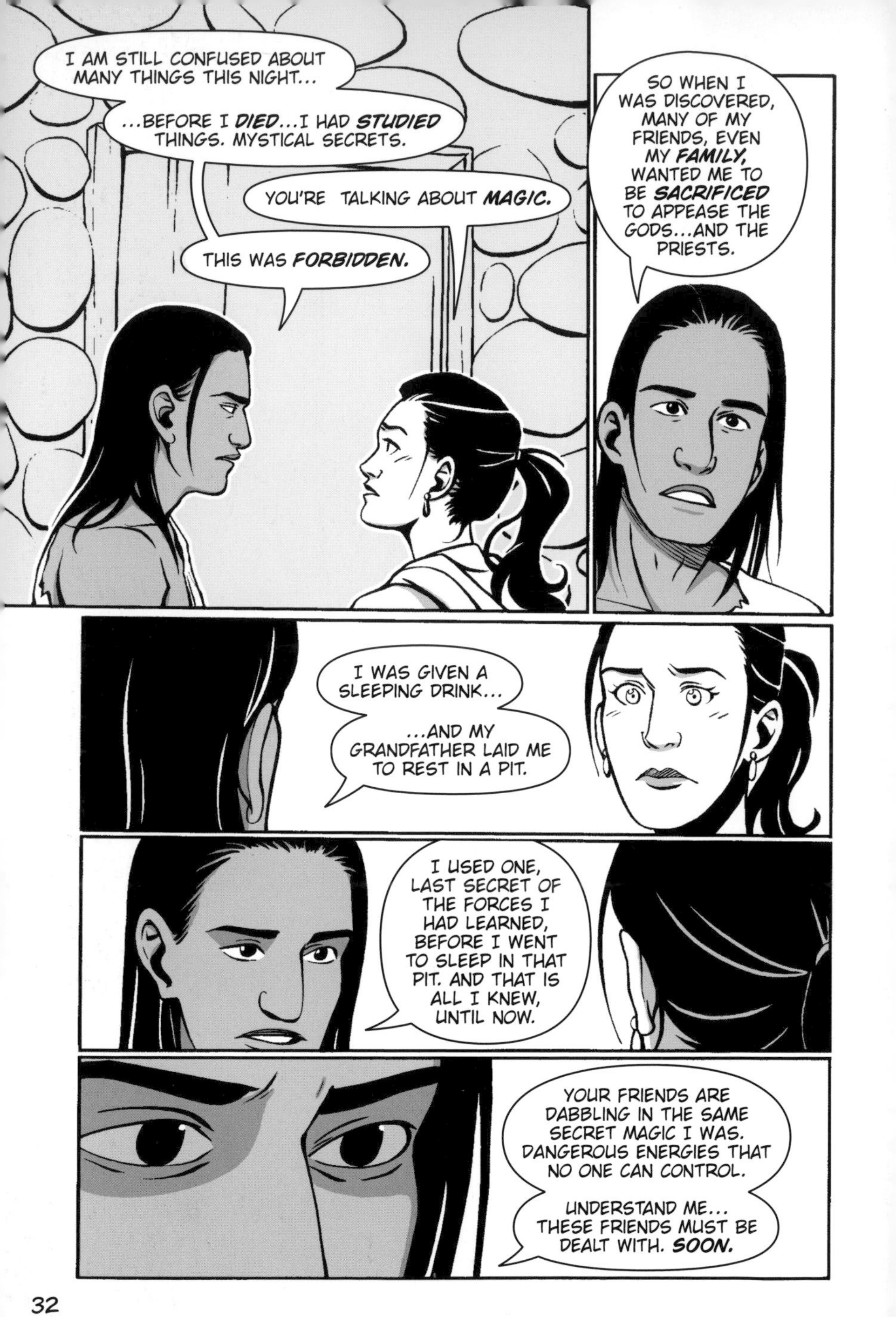
I AM STILL CONFUSED ABOUT MANY THINGS THIS NIGHT...
...BEFORE I *DIED*...I HAD *STUDIED* THINGS. MYSTICAL SECRETS.
YOU'RE TALKING ABOUT *MAGIC.*
THIS WAS *FORBIDDEN.*
SO WHEN I WAS DISCOVERED, MANY OF MY FRIENDS, EVEN MY *FAMILY,* WANTED ME TO BE *SACRIFICED* TO APPEASE THE GODS...AND THE PRIESTS.
I WAS GIVEN A SLEEPING DRINK...
...AND MY GRANDFATHER LAID ME TO REST IN A PIT.
I USED ONE, LAST SECRET OF THE FORCES I HAD LEARNED, BEFORE I WENT TO SLEEP IN THAT PIT. AND THAT IS ALL I KNEW, UNTIL NOW.
YOUR FRIENDS ARE DABBLING IN THE SAME SECRET MAGIC I WAS. DANGEROUS ENERGIES THAT NO ONE CAN CONTROL.
UNDERSTAND ME... THESE FRIENDS MUST BE DEALT WITH. *SOON.*

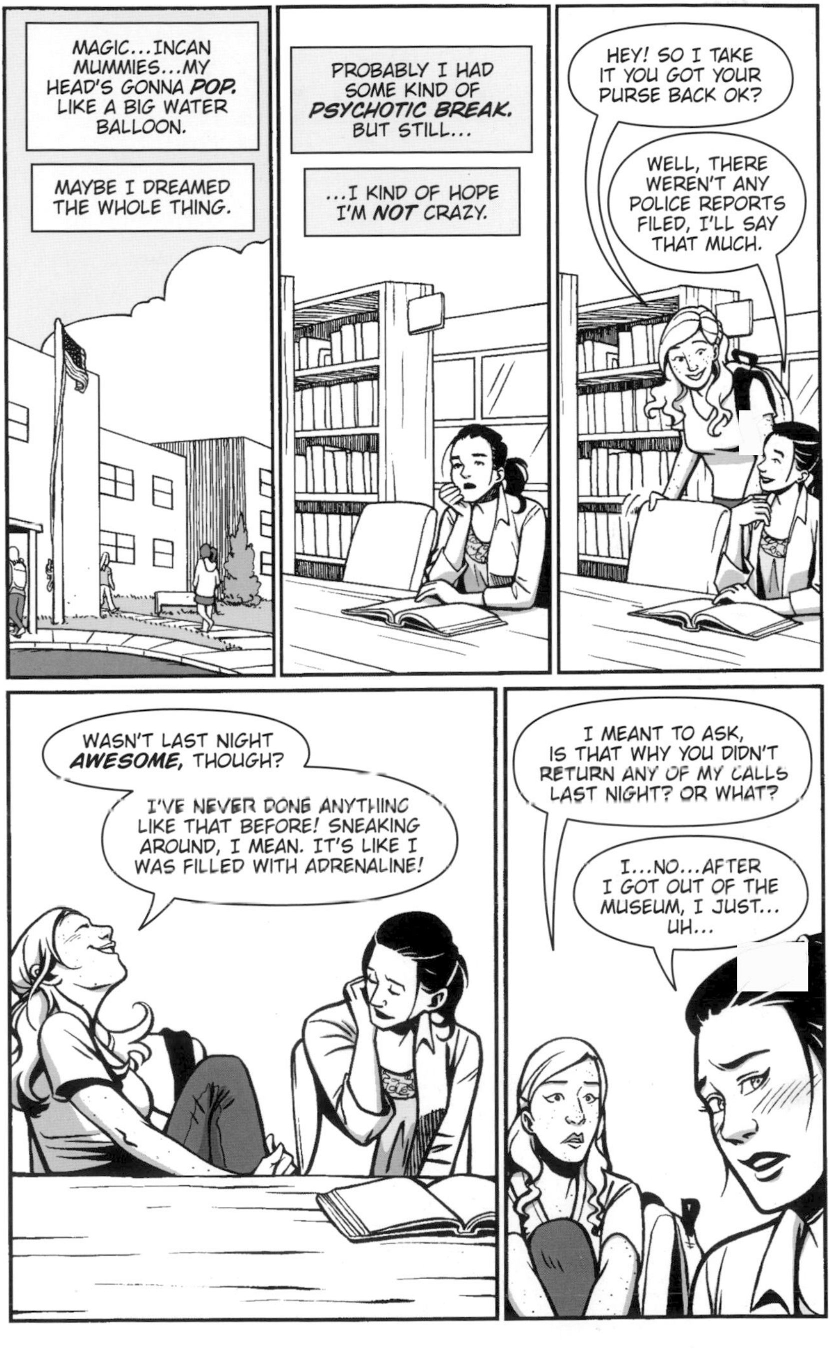
MAGIC...INCAN MUMMIES...MY HEAD'S GONNA **POP.** LIKE A BIG WATER BALLOON.
MAYBE I DREAMED THE WHOLE THING.
PROBABLY I HAD SOME KIND OF **PSYCHOTIC BREAK.** BUT STILL...
...I KIND OF HOPE I'M **NOT** CRAZY.
HEY! SO I TAKE IT YOU GOT YOUR PURSE BACK OK?
WELL, THERE WEREN'T ANY POLICE REPORTS FILED, I'LL SAY THAT MUCH.
WASN'T LAST NIGHT **AWESOME,** THOUGH?
I'VE NEVER DONE ANYTHING LIKE THAT BEFORE! SNEAKING AROUND, I MEAN. IT'S LIKE I WAS FILLED WITH ADRENALINE!
I MEANT TO ASK, IS THAT WHY YOU DIDN'T RETURN ANY OF MY CALLS LAST NIGHT? OR WHAT?
I...NO...AFTER I GOT OUT OF THE MUSEUM, I JUST... UH...

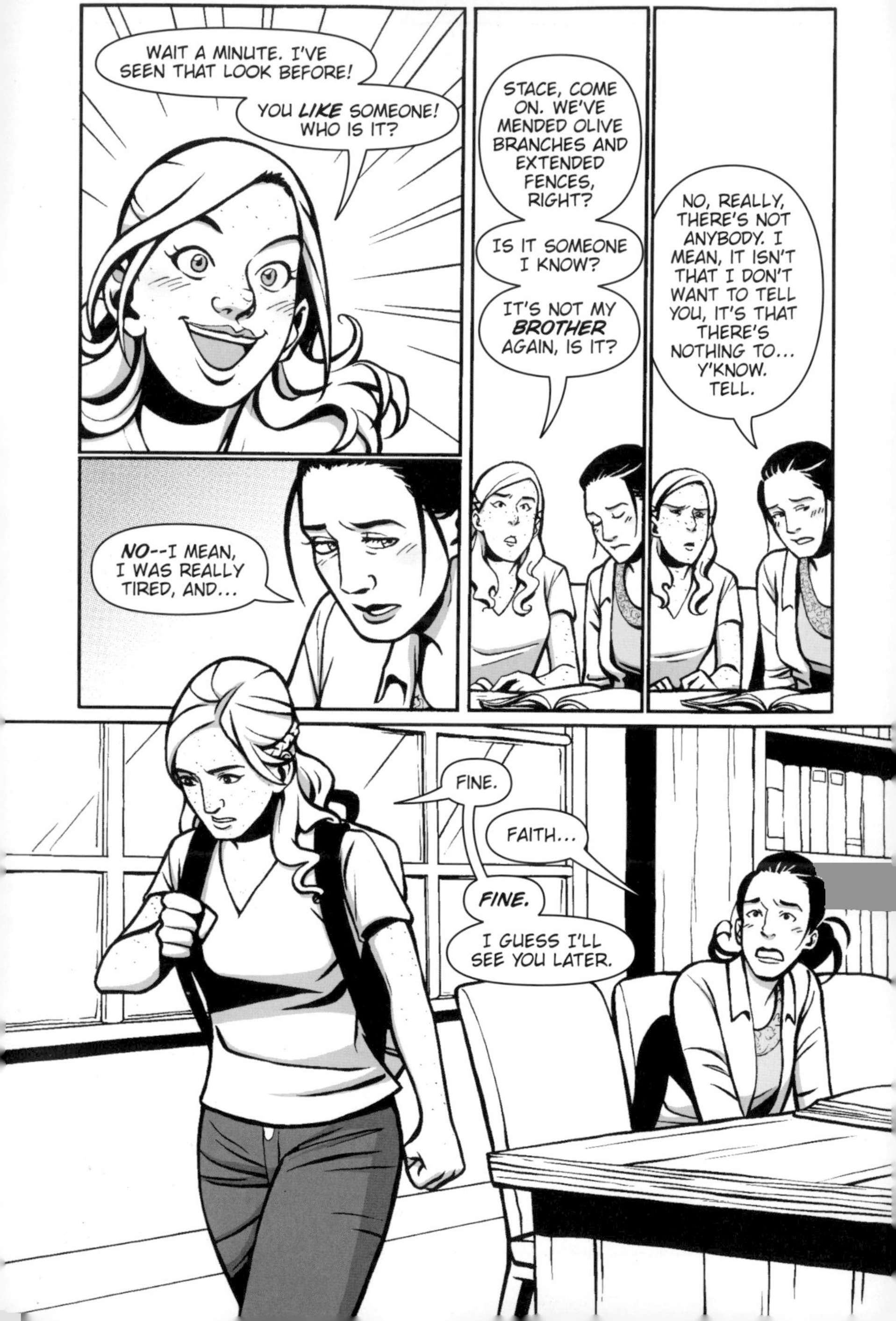

WAIT A MINUTE. I'VE SEEN THAT LOOK BEFORE!
YOU ***LIKE*** SOMEONE! WHO IS IT?
STACE, COME ON. WE'VE MENDED OLIVE BRANCHES AND EXTENDED FENCES, RIGHT?
IS IT SOMEONE I KNOW?
IT'S NOT MY ***BROTHER*** AGAIN, IS IT?
NO, REALLY, THERE'S NOT ANYBODY. I MEAN, IT ISN'T THAT I DON'T WANT TO TELL YOU, IT'S THAT THERE'S NOTHING TO... Y'KNOW. TELL.
NO--I MEAN, I WAS REALLY TIRED, AND...
FINE.
FAITH...
FINE.
I GUESS I'LL SEE YOU LATER.

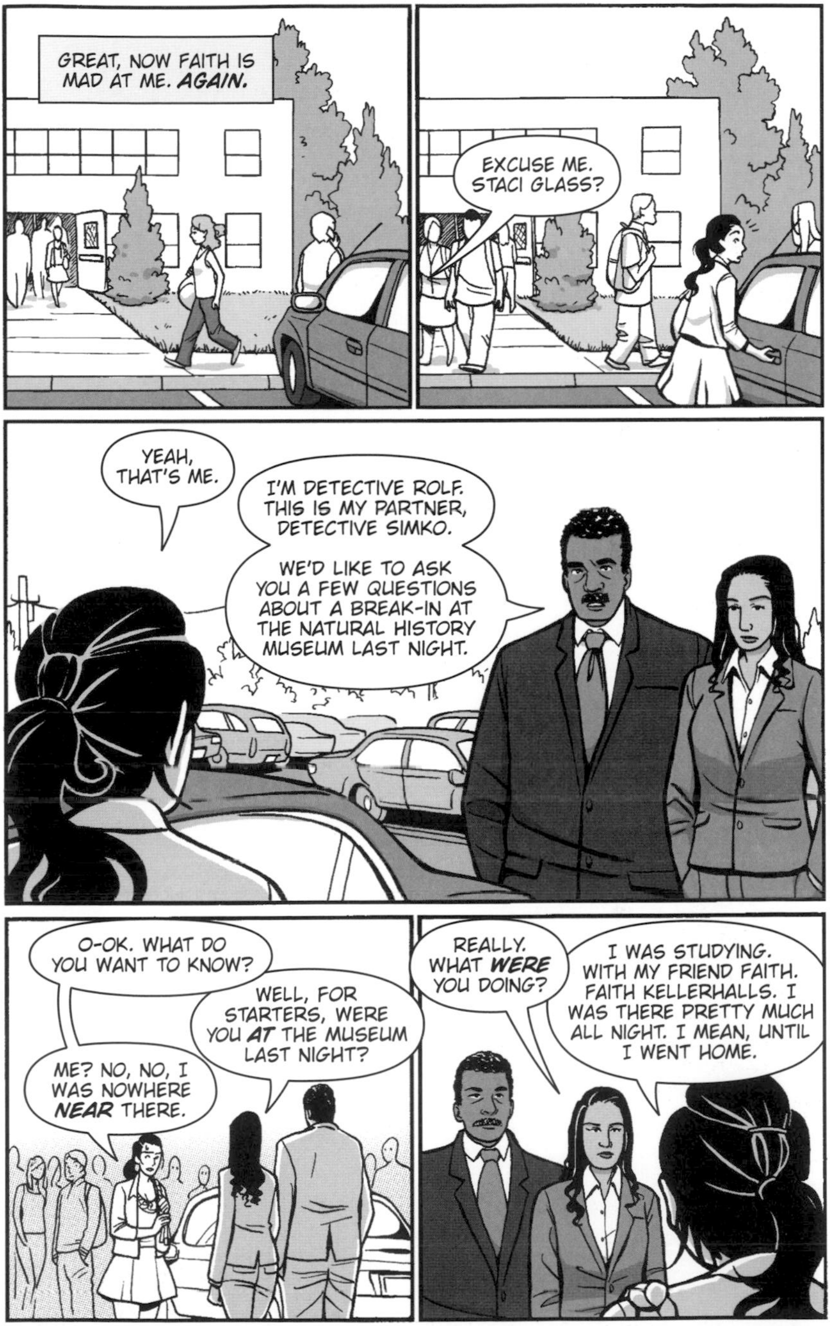
GREAT, NOW FAITH IS MAD AT ME. ***AGAIN.***
EXCUSE ME. STACI GLASS?
YEAH, THAT'S ME.
I'M DETECTIVE ROLF. THIS IS MY PARTNER, DETECTIVE SIMKO.
WE'D LIKE TO ASK YOU A FEW QUESTIONS ABOUT A BREAK-IN AT THE NATURAL HISTORY MUSEUM LAST NIGHT.
O-OK. WHAT DO YOU WANT TO KNOW?
WELL, FOR STARTERS, WERE YOU ***AT*** THE MUSEUM LAST NIGHT?
ME? NO, NO, I WAS NOWHERE ***NEAR*** THERE.
REALLY. WHAT ***WERE*** YOU DOING?
I WAS STUDYING. WITH MY FRIEND FAITH. FAITH KELLERHALLS. I WAS THERE PRETTY MUCH ALL NIGHT. I MEAN, UNTIL I WENT HOME.

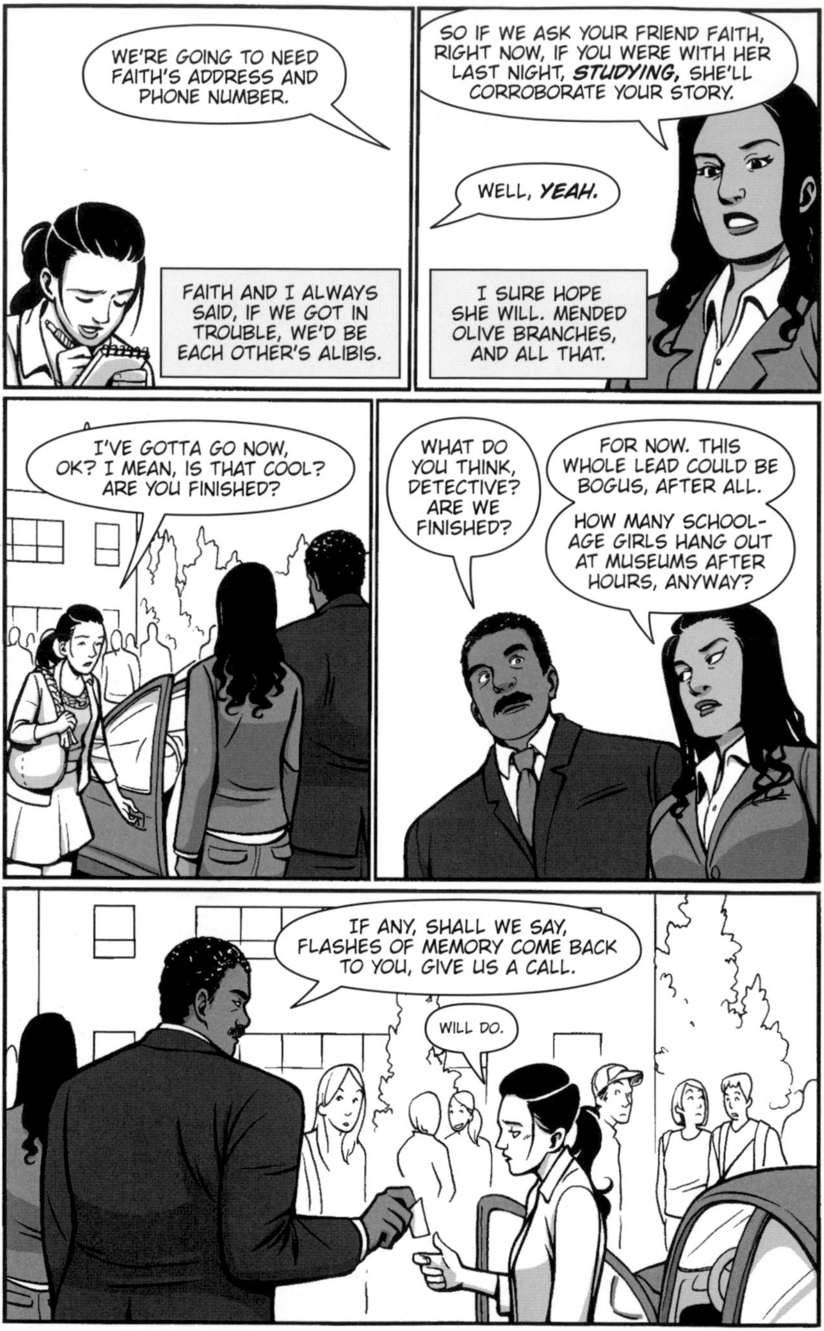
WE'RE GOING TO NEED FAITH'S ADDRESS AND PHONE NUMBER.
FAITH AND I ALWAYS SAID, IF WE GOT IN TROUBLE, WE'D BE EACH OTHER'S ALIBIS.
SO IF WE ASK YOUR FRIEND FAITH, RIGHT NOW, IF YOU WERE WITH HER LAST NIGHT, *STUDYING,* SHE'LL CORROBORATE YOUR STORY.
WELL, *YEAH.*
I SURE HOPE SHE WILL. MENDED OLIVE BRANCHES, AND ALL THAT.
I'VE GOTTA GO NOW, OK? I MEAN, IS THAT COOL? ARE YOU FINISHED?
WHAT DO YOU THINK, DETECTIVE? ARE WE FINISHED?
FOR NOW. THIS WHOLE LEAD COULD BE BOGUS, AFTER ALL.
HOW MANY SCHOOL-AGE GIRLS HANG OUT AT MUSEUMS AFTER HOURS, ANYWAY?
IF ANY, SHALL WE SAY, FLASHES OF MEMORY COME BACK TO YOU, GIVE US A CALL.
WILL DO.

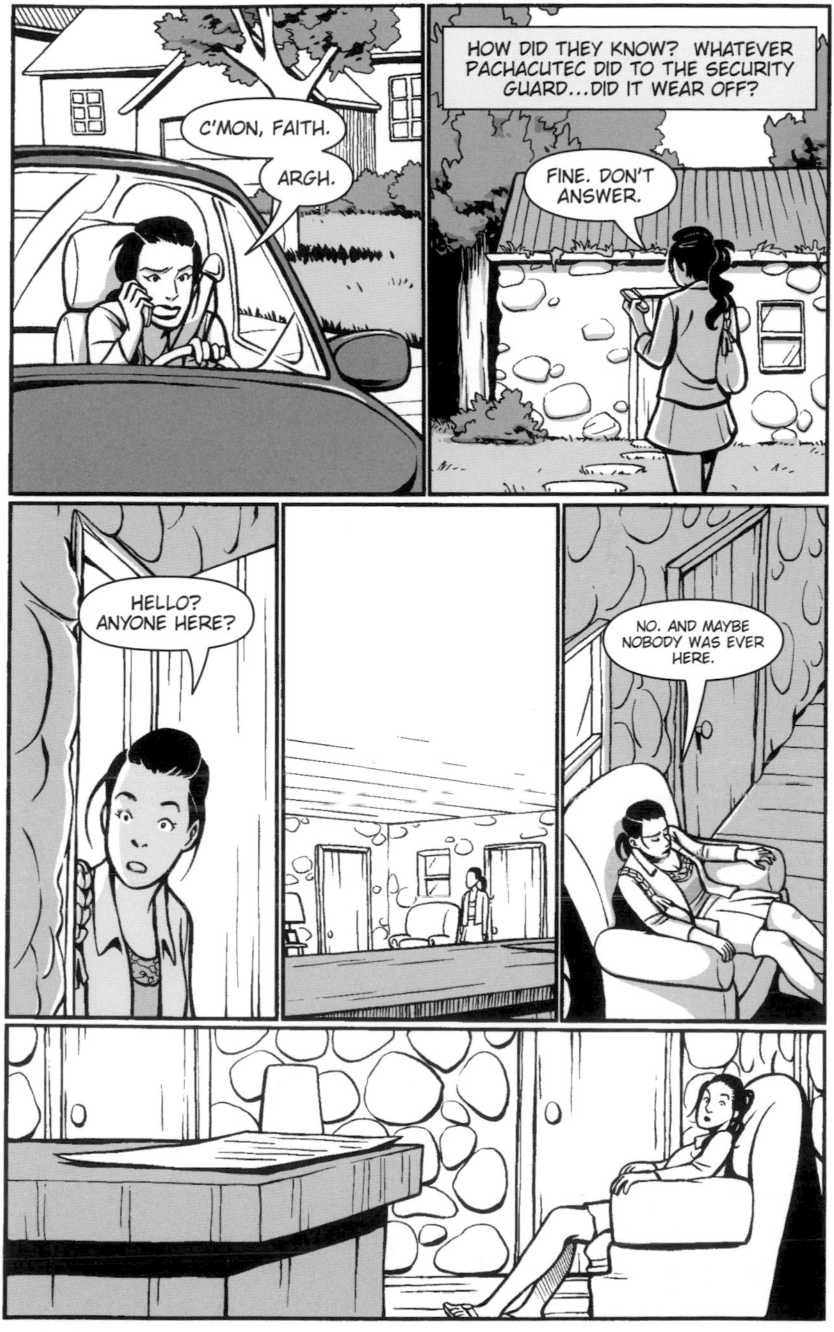
C'MON, FAITH.
ARGH.
HOW DID THEY KNOW? WHATEVER PACHACUTEC DID TO THE SECURITY GUARD...DID IT WEAR OFF?
FINE. DON'T ANSWER.
HELLO? ANYONE HERE?
NO. AND MAYBE NOBODY WAS EVER HERE.

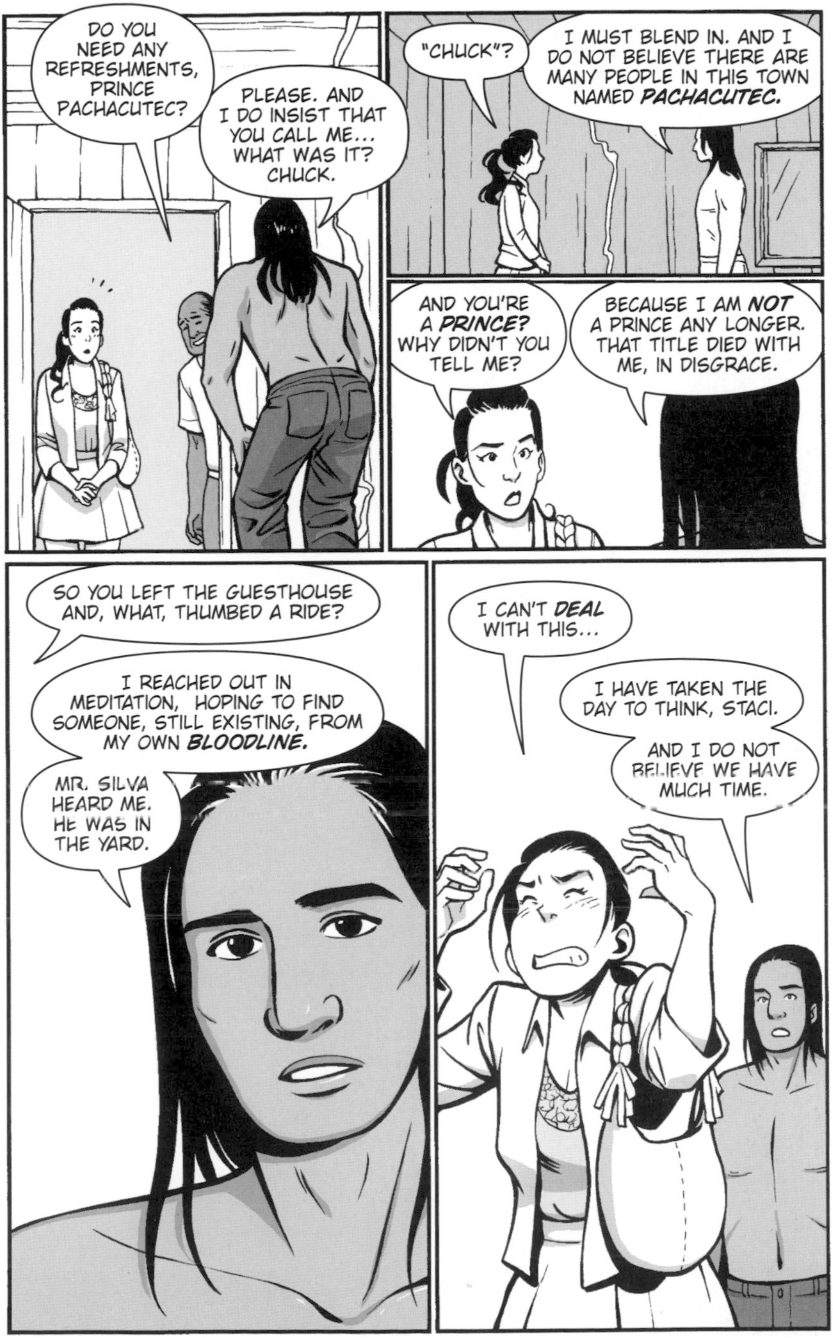
DO YOU NEED ANY REFRESHMENTS, PRINCE PACHACUTEC?
PLEASE. AND I DO INSIST THAT YOU CALL ME... WHAT WAS IT? CHUCK.
"CHUCK"?
I MUST BLEND IN. AND I DO NOT BELIEVE THERE ARE MANY PEOPLE IN THIS TOWN NAMED *PACHACUTEC.*
AND YOU'RE A *PRINCE?* WHY DIDN'T YOU TELL ME?
BECAUSE I AM *NOT* A PRINCE ANY LONGER. THAT TITLE DIED WITH ME, IN DISGRACE.
SO YOU LEFT THE GUESTHOUSE AND, WHAT, THUMBED A RIDE?
I REACHED OUT IN MEDITATION, HOPING TO FIND SOMEONE, STILL EXISTING, FROM MY OWN *BLOODLINE.*
MR. SILVA HEARD ME. HE WAS IN THE YARD.
I CAN'T *DEAL* WITH THIS...
I HAVE TAKEN THE DAY TO THINK, STACI.
AND I DO NOT BELIEVE WE HAVE MUCH TIME.

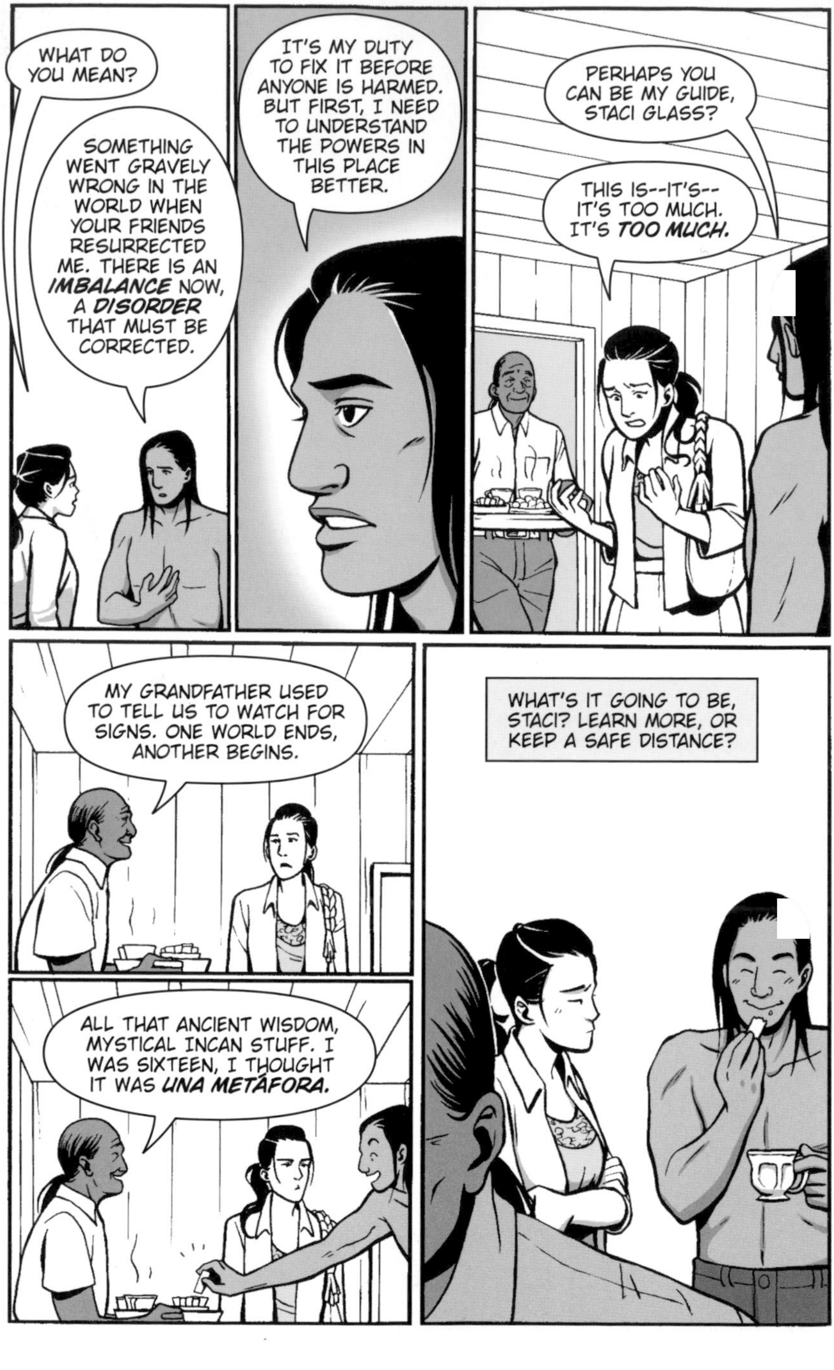
WHAT DO YOU MEAN?
SOMETHING WENT GRAVELY WRONG IN THE WORLD WHEN YOUR FRIENDS RESURRECTED ME. THERE IS AN *IMBALANCE* NOW, A *DISORDER* THAT MUST BE CORRECTED.
IT'S MY DUTY TO FIX IT BEFORE ANYONE IS HARMED. BUT FIRST, I NEED TO UNDERSTAND THE POWERS IN THIS PLACE BETTER.
PERHAPS YOU CAN BE MY GUIDE, STACI GLASS?
THIS IS--IT'S--IT'S TOO MUCH. IT'S ***TOO MUCH.***
MY GRANDFATHER USED TO TELL US TO WATCH FOR SIGNS. ONE WORLD ENDS, ANOTHER BEGINS.
ALL THAT ANCIENT WISDOM, MYSTICAL INCAN STUFF. I WAS SIXTEEN, I THOUGHT IT WAS ***UNA METÁFORA.***
WHAT'S IT GOING TO BE, STACI? LEARN MORE, OR KEEP A SAFE DISTANCE?

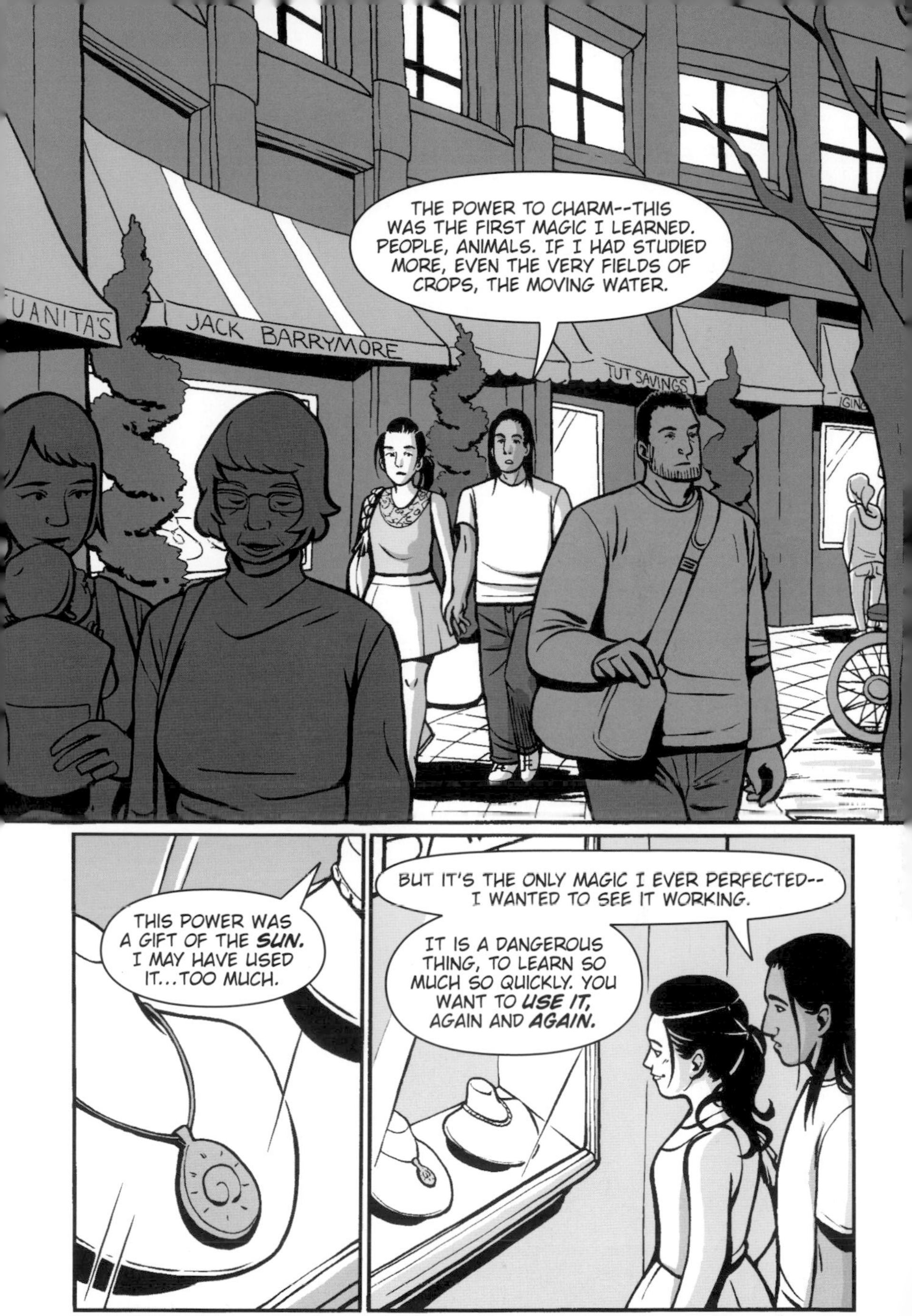
UANITA'S
JACK BARRYMORE
TUT SAVINGS
THE POWER TO CHARM--THIS WAS THE FIRST MAGIC I LEARNED. PEOPLE, ANIMALS. IF I HAD STUDIED MORE, EVEN THE VERY FIELDS OF CROPS, THE MOVING WATER.
THIS POWER WAS A GIFT OF THE ***SUN.*** I MAY HAVE USED IT...TOO MUCH.
BUT IT'S THE ONLY MAGIC I EVER PERFECTED-- I WANTED TO SEE IT WORKING.
IT IS A DANGEROUS THING, TO LEARN SO MUCH SO QUICKLY. YOU WANT TO ***USE IT,*** AGAIN AND ***AGAIN.***

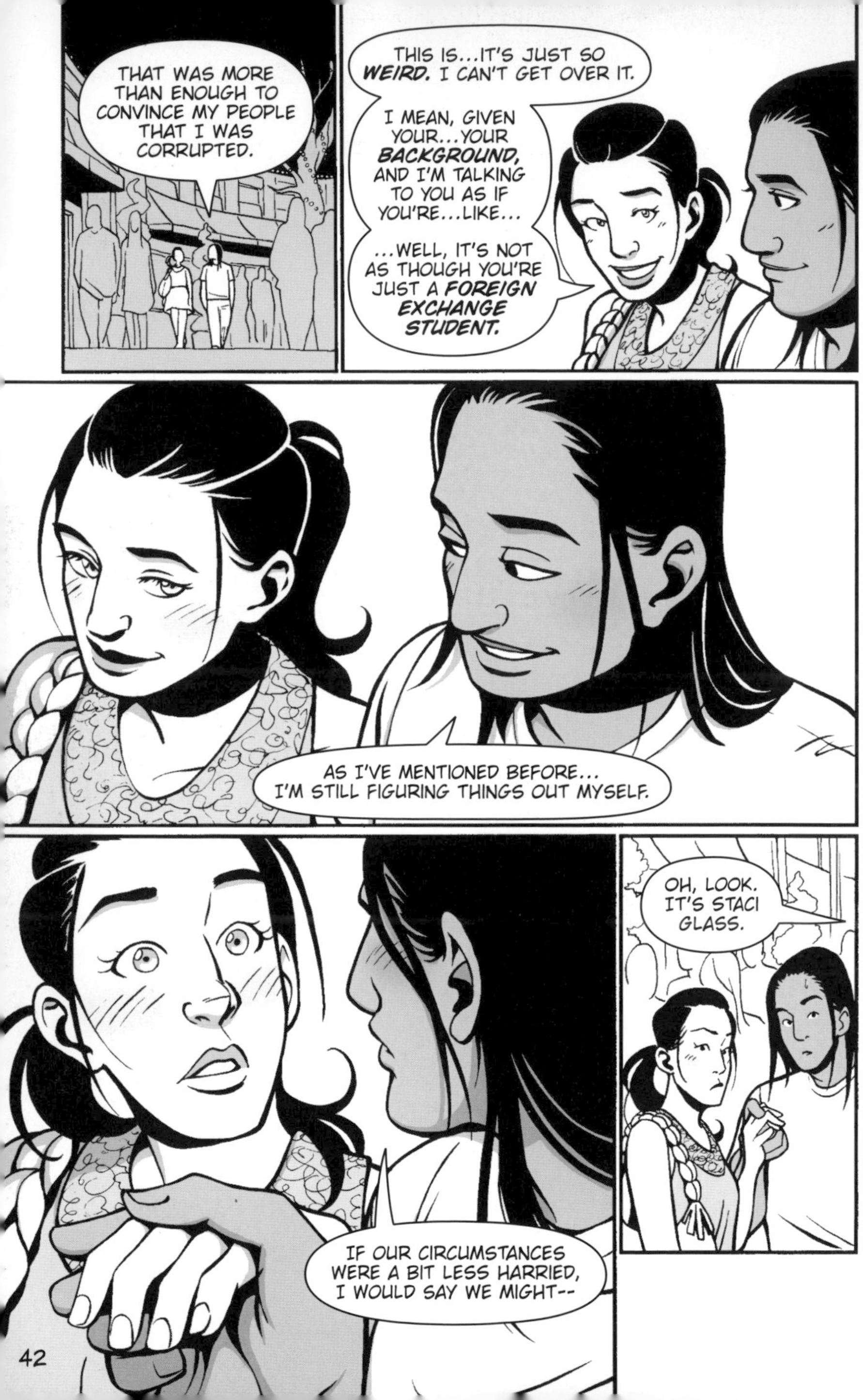
THAT WAS MORE THAN ENOUGH TO CONVINCE MY PEOPLE THAT I WAS CORRUPTED.
THIS IS...IT'S JUST SO WEIRD. I CAN'T GET OVER IT.
I MEAN, GIVEN YOUR...YOUR BACKGROUND, AND I'M TALKING TO YOU AS IF YOU'RE...LIKE...
...WELL, IT'S NOT AS THOUGH YOU'RE JUST A FOREIGN EXCHANGE STUDENT.
AS I'VE MENTIONED BEFORE... I'M STILL FIGURING THINGS OUT MYSELF.
IF OUR CIRCUMSTANCES WERE A BIT LESS HARRIED, I WOULD SAY WE MIGHT--
OH, LOOK. IT'S STACI GLASS.

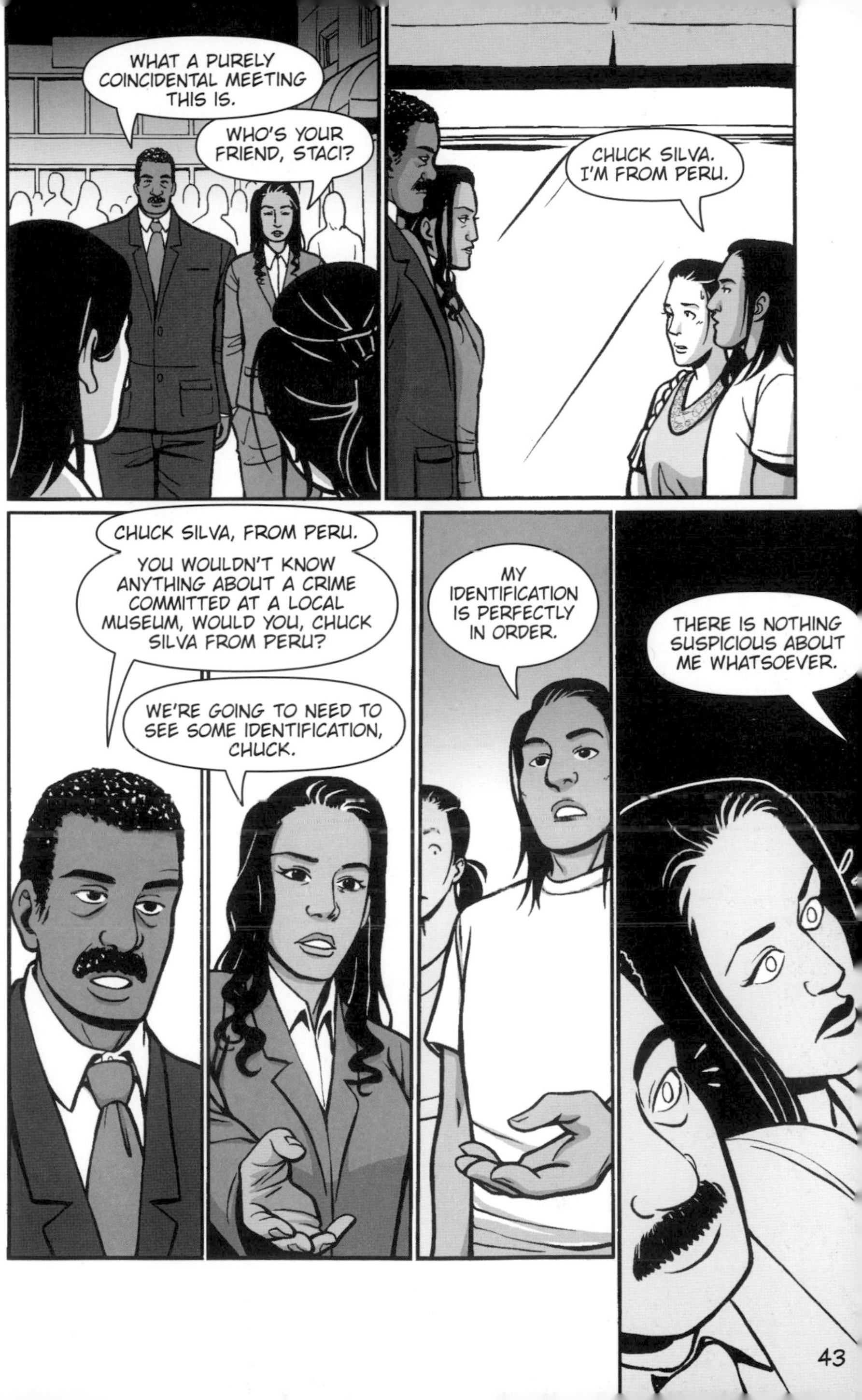
WHAT A PURELY COINCIDENTAL MEETING THIS IS.
WHO'S YOUR FRIEND, STACI?
CHUCK SILVA. I'M FROM PERU.
CHUCK SILVA, FROM PERU.
YOU WOULDN'T KNOW ANYTHING ABOUT A CRIME COMMITTED AT A LOCAL MUSEUM, WOULD YOU, CHUCK SILVA FROM PERU?
WE'RE GOING TO NEED TO SEE SOME IDENTIFICATION, CHUCK.
MY IDENTIFICATION IS PERFECTLY IN ORDER.
THERE IS NOTHING SUSPICIOUS ABOUT ME WHATSOEVER.

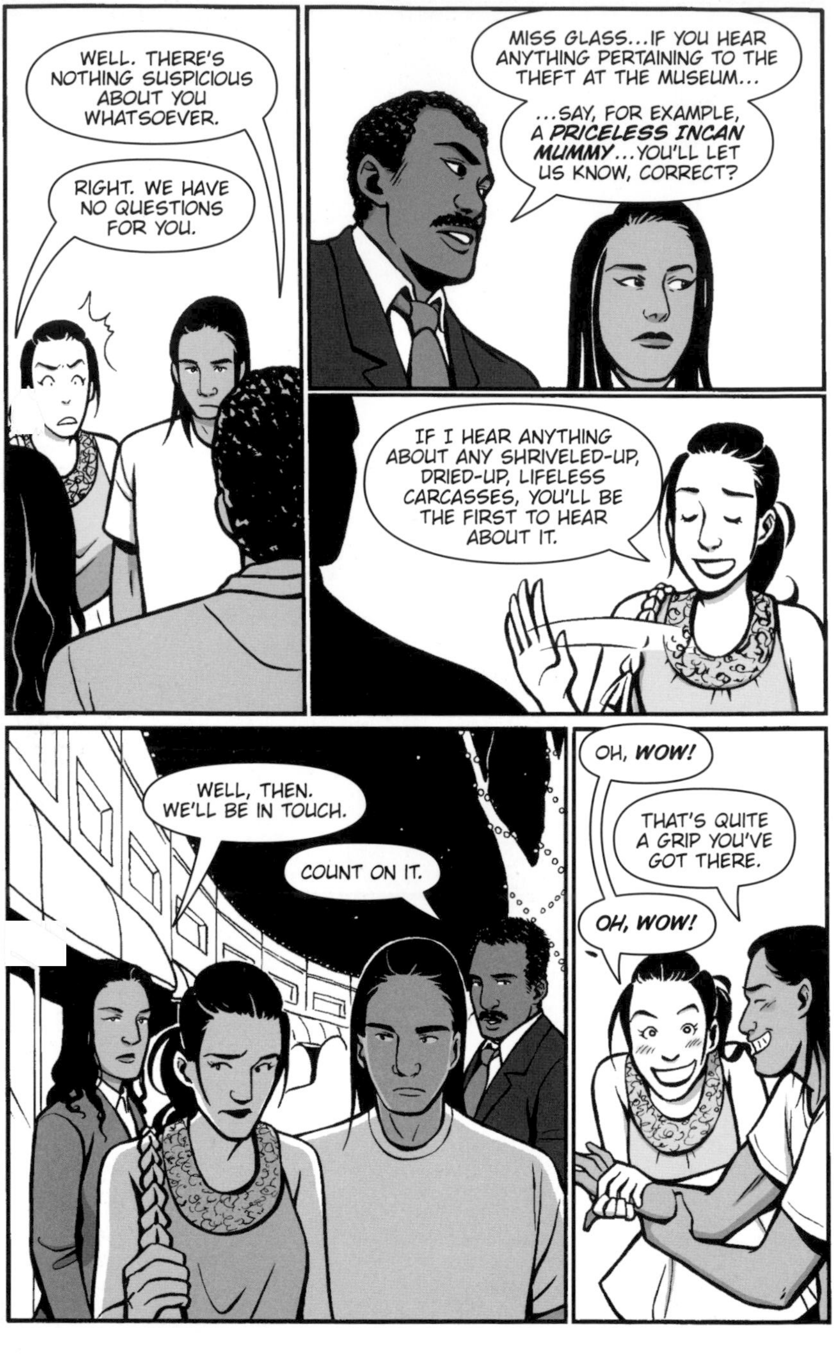
WELL. THERE'S NOTHING SUSPICIOUS ABOUT YOU WHATSOEVER.
RIGHT. WE HAVE NO QUESTIONS FOR YOU.
MISS GLASS...IF YOU HEAR ANYTHING PERTAINING TO THE THEFT AT THE MUSEUM...
...SAY, FOR EXAMPLE, A PRICELESS INCAN MUMMY...YOU'LL LET US KNOW, CORRECT?
IF I HEAR ANYTHING ABOUT ANY SHRIVELED-UP, DRIED-UP, LIFELESS CARCASSES, YOU'LL BE THE FIRST TO HEAR ABOUT IT.
WELL, THEN. WE'LL BE IN TOUCH.
COUNT ON IT.
OH, WOW!
THAT'S QUITE A GRIP YOU'VE GOT THERE.
OH, WOW!

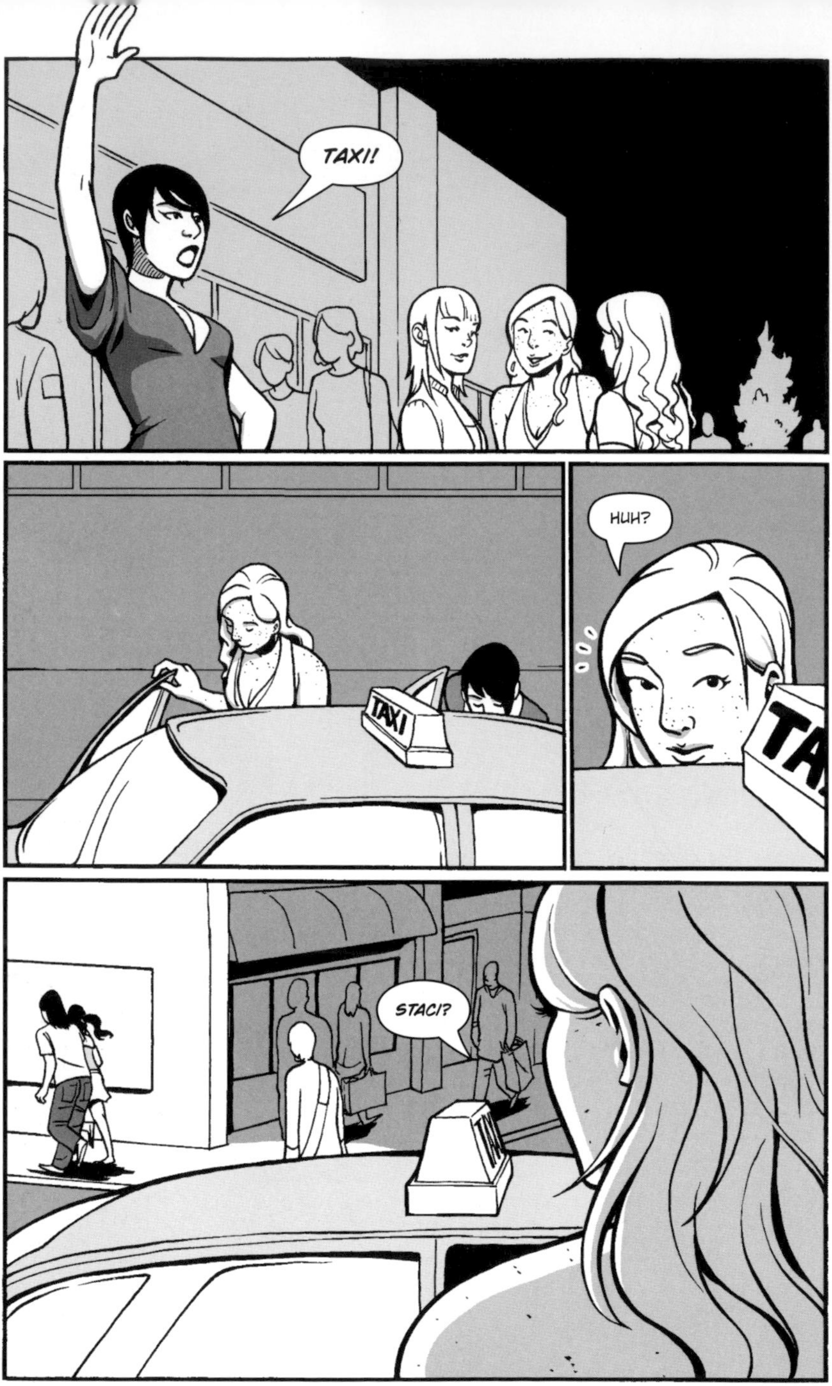
TAXI!
TAXI
HUH?
TAXI
STACI?

49

51

52

CHAPTER THREE

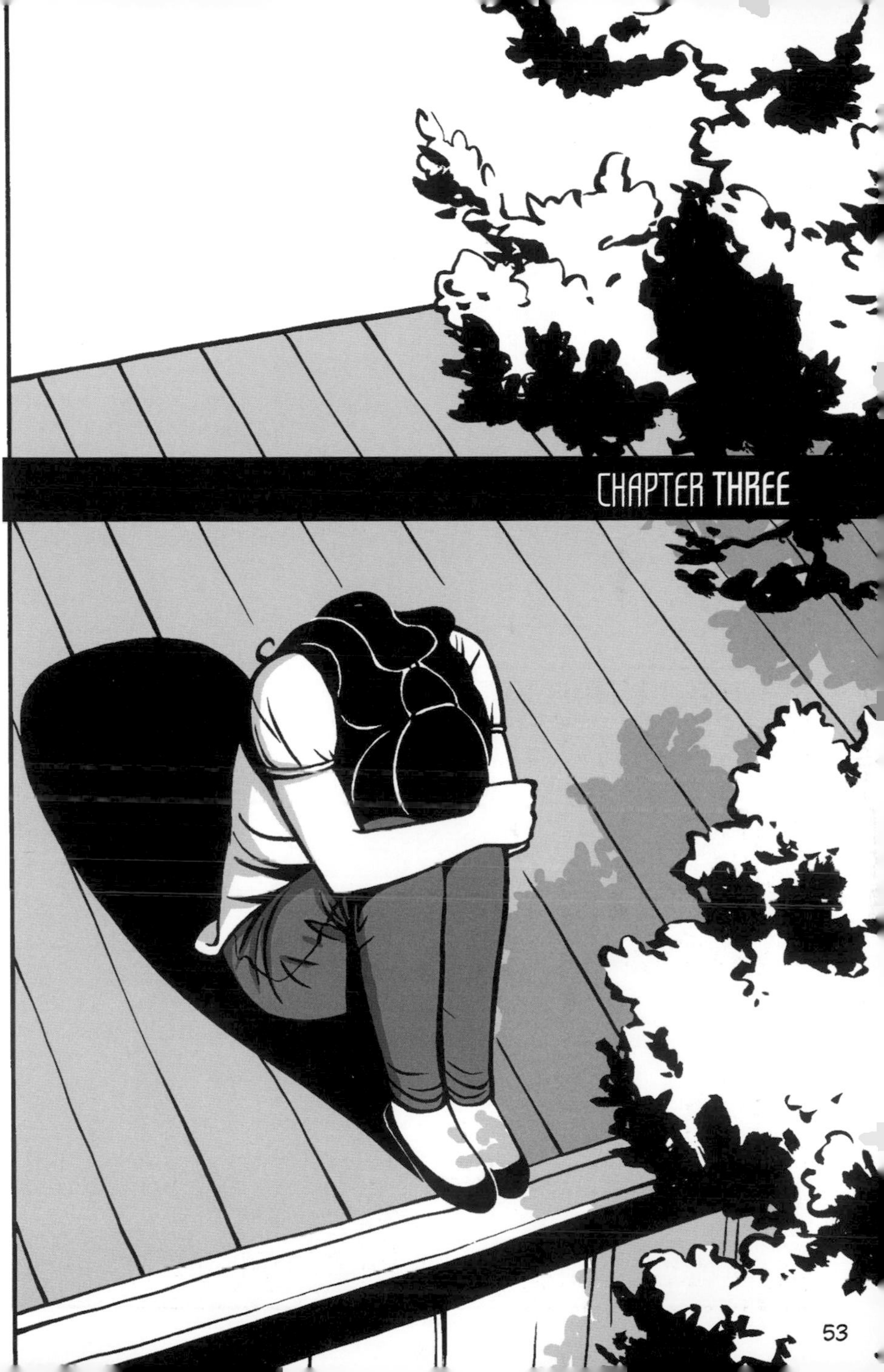

WILL SHE EVEN WANT TO TALK TO ME?

IF YOU'D LIKE TO LEAVE A MESSAGE—

GUESS NOT.

FAITH

CALL

55

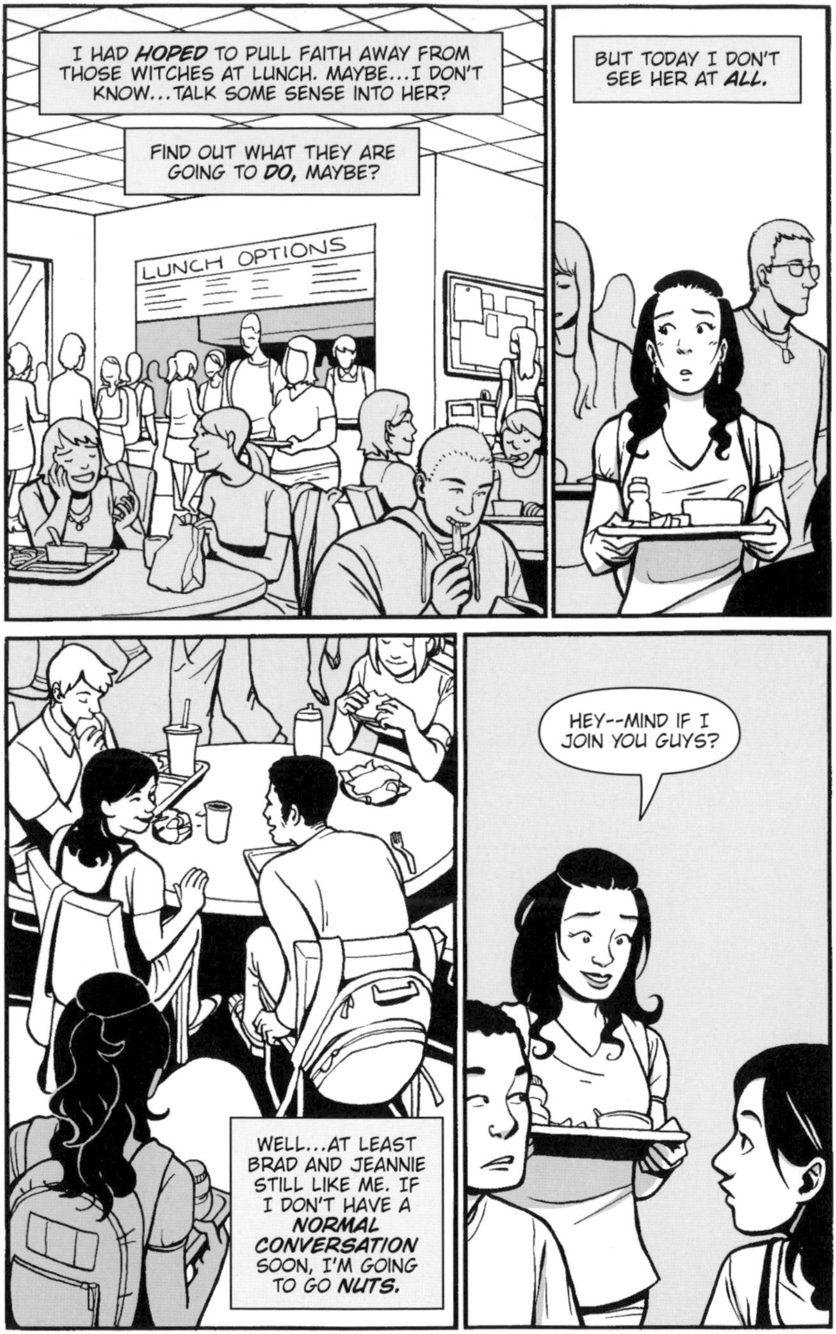

I HAD HOPED TO PULL FAITH AWAY FROM THOSE WITCHES AT LUNCH. MAYBE...I DON'T KNOW...TALK SOME SENSE INTO HER?
FIND OUT WHAT THEY ARE GOING TO DO, MAYBE?
LUNCH OPTIONS
BUT TODAY I DON'T SEE HER AT ALL.
WELL...AT LEAST BRAD AND JEANNIE STILL LIKE ME. IF I DON'T HAVE A NORMAL CONVERSATION SOON, I'M GOING TO GO NUTS.
HEY--MIND IF I JOIN YOU GUYS?

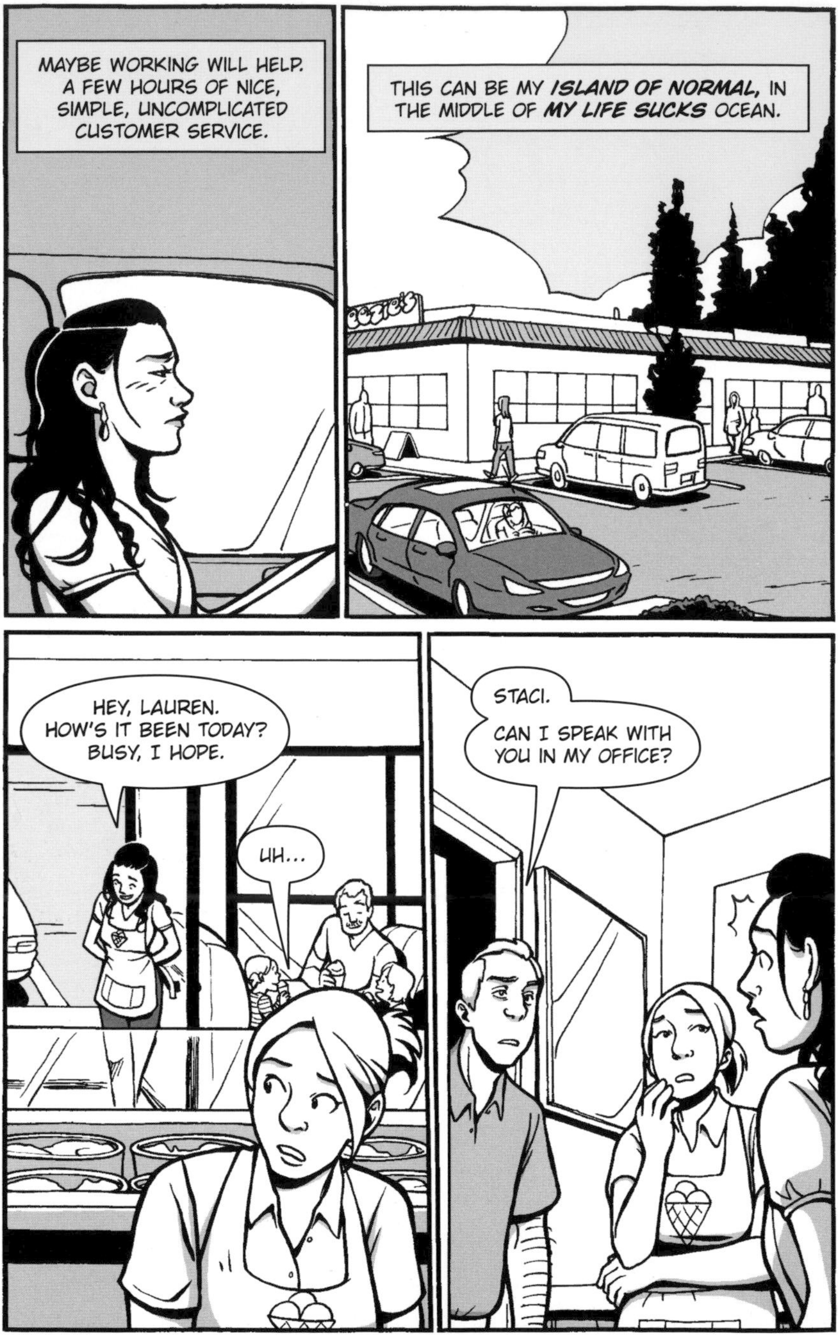
MAYBE WORKING WILL HELP. A FEW HOURS OF NICE, SIMPLE, UNCOMPLICATED CUSTOMER SERVICE.
THIS CAN BE MY ***ISLAND OF NORMAL,*** IN THE MIDDLE OF ***MY LIFE SUCKS*** OCEAN.
HEY, LAUREN. HOW'S IT BEEN TODAY? BUSY, I HOPE.
UH...
STACI.
CAN I SPEAK WITH YOU IN MY OFFICE?

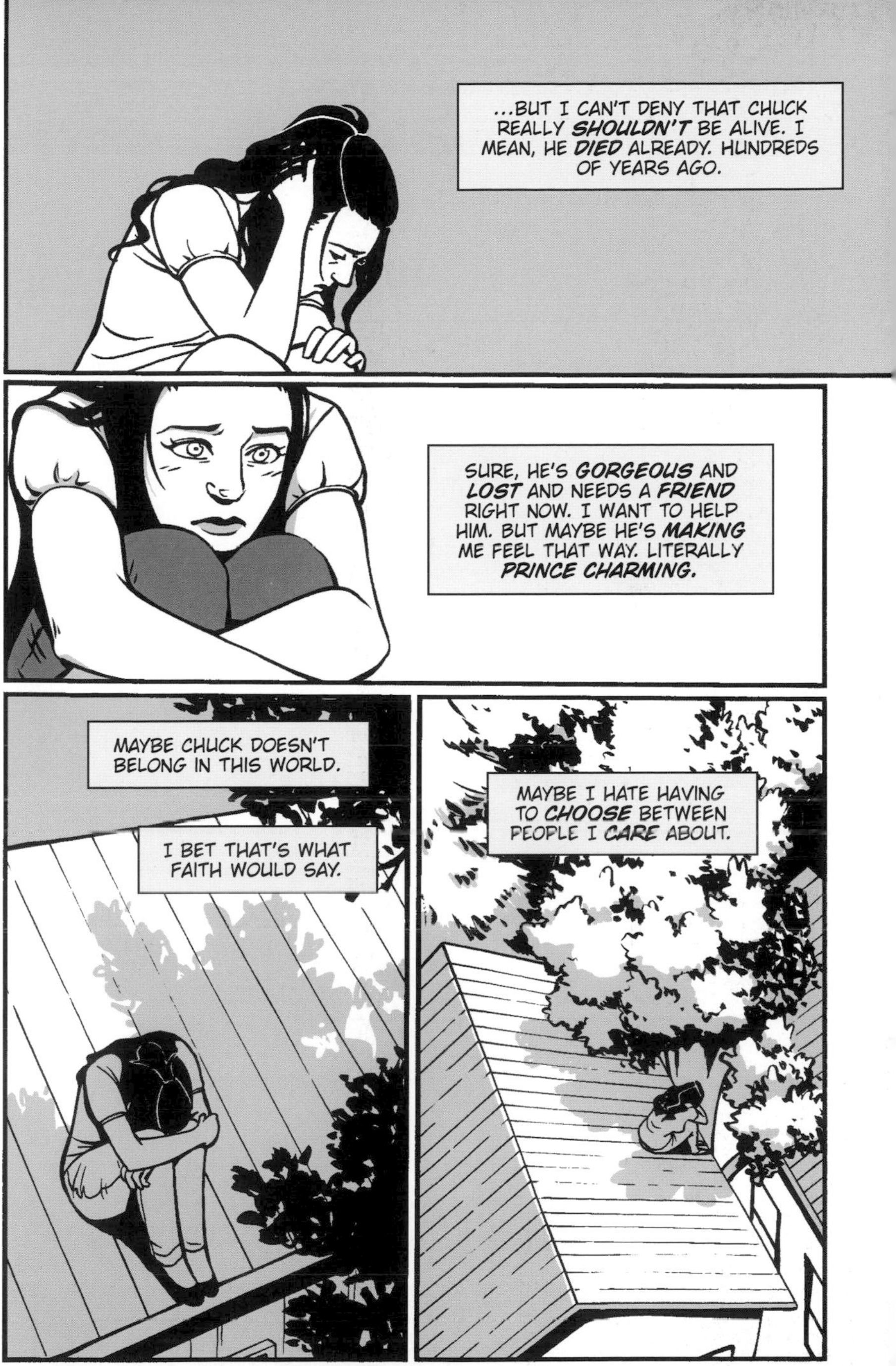
...BUT I CAN'T DENY THAT CHUCK REALLY SHOULDN'T BE ALIVE. I MEAN, HE DIED ALREADY. HUNDREDS OF YEARS AGO.
SURE, HE'S GORGEOUS AND LOST AND NEEDS A FRIEND RIGHT NOW. I WANT TO HELP HIM. BUT MAYBE HE'S MAKING ME FEEL THAT WAY. LITERALLY PRINCE CHARMING.
MAYBE CHUCK DOESN'T BELONG IN THIS WORLD.
I BET THAT'S WHAT FAITH WOULD SAY.
MAYBE I HATE HAVING TO CHOOSE BETWEEN PEOPLE I CARE ABOUT.

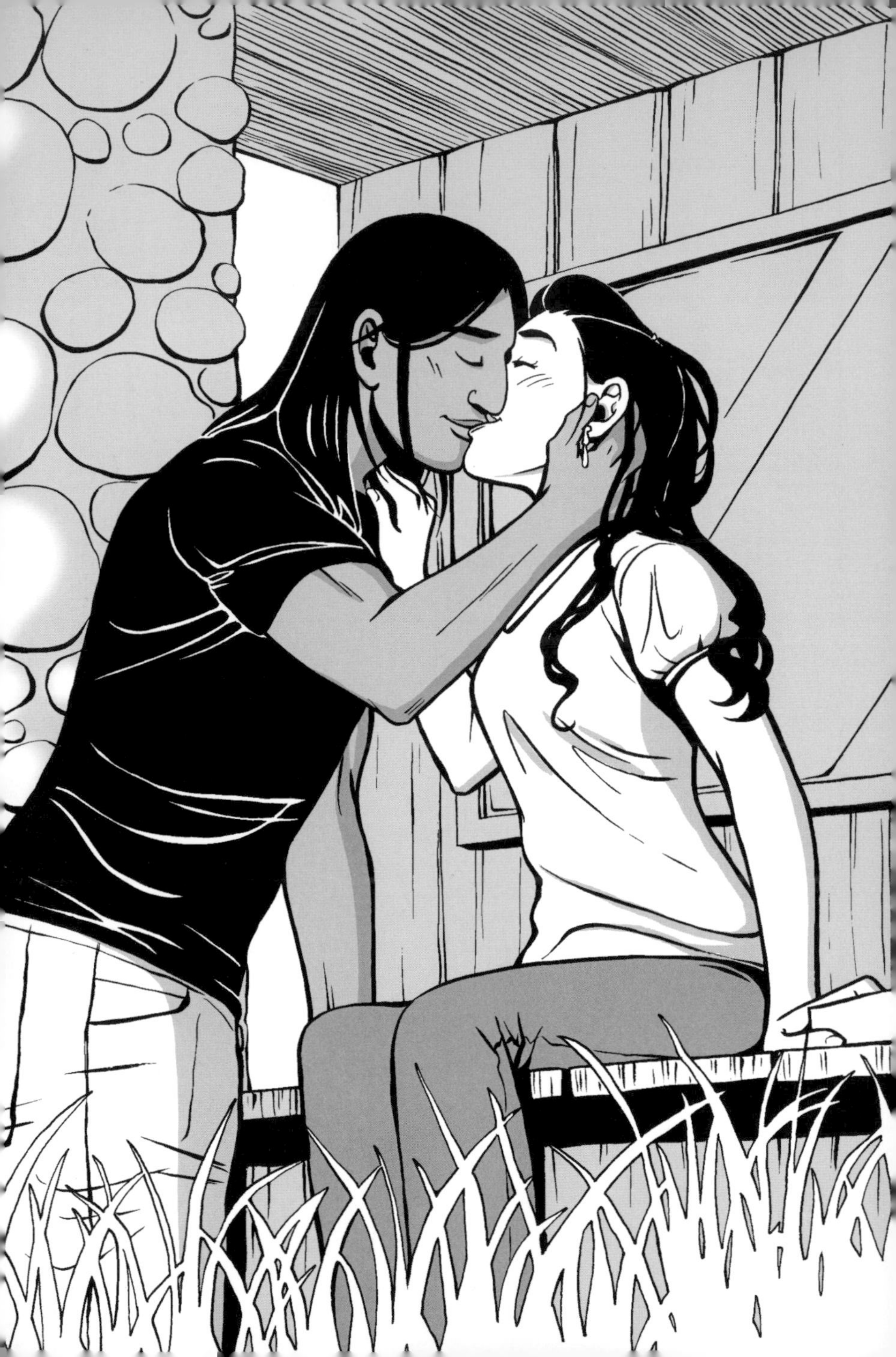

73

CHAPTER FOUR

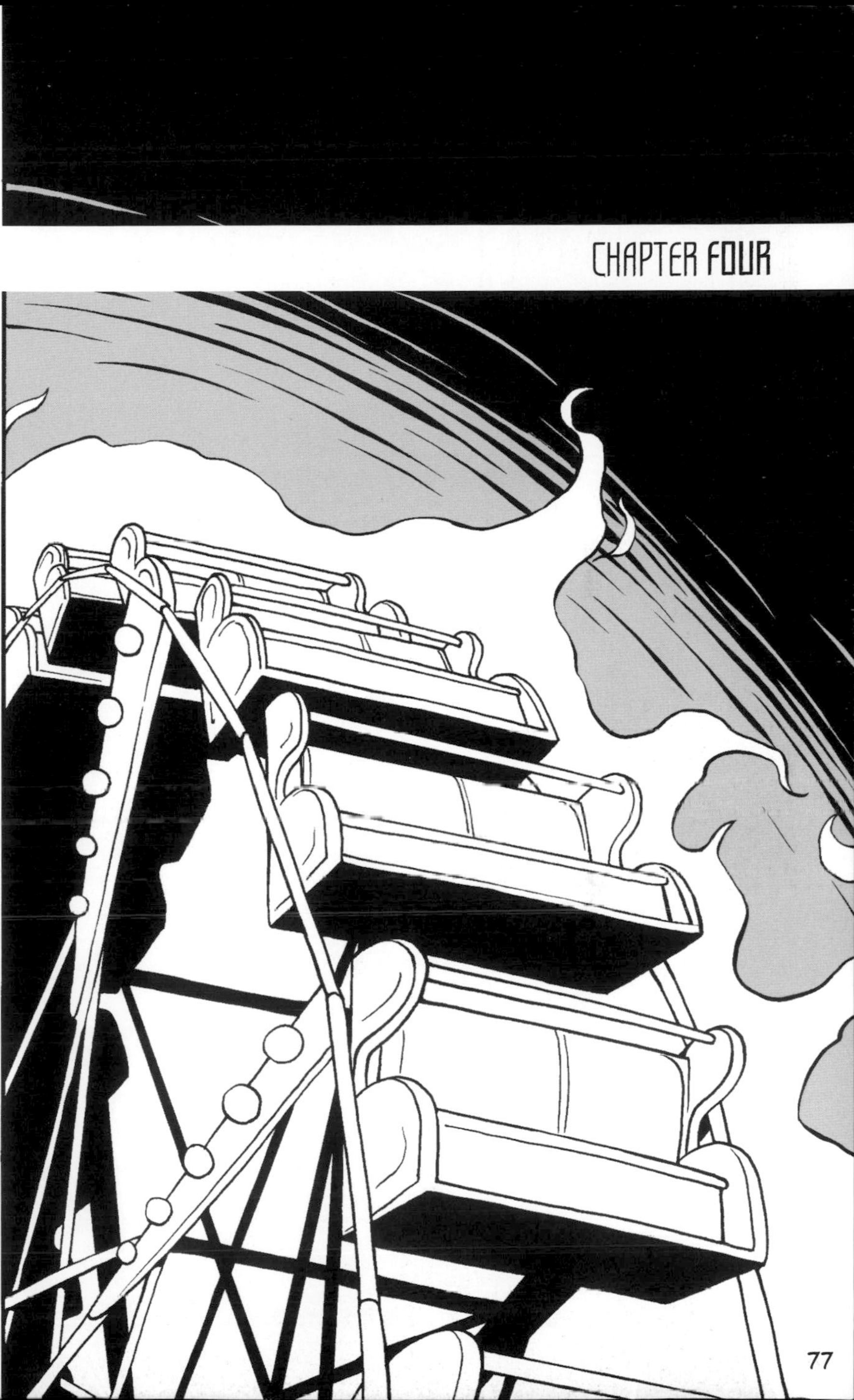

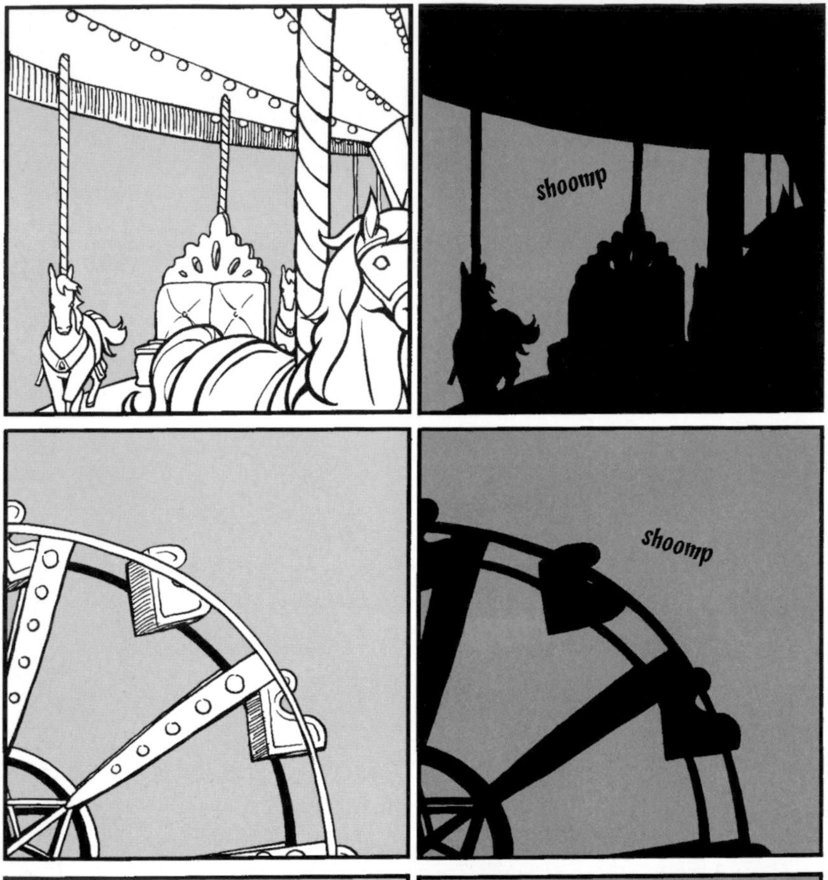
shoomp
shoomp
shoomp
IT FEELS AS IF EVERYTHING IS COMING TO A HEAD.

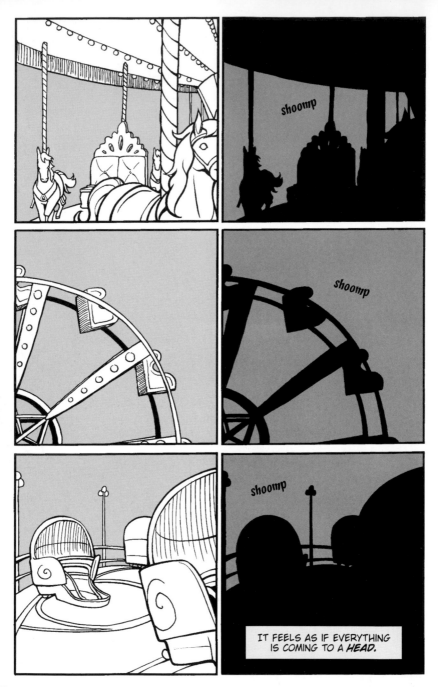

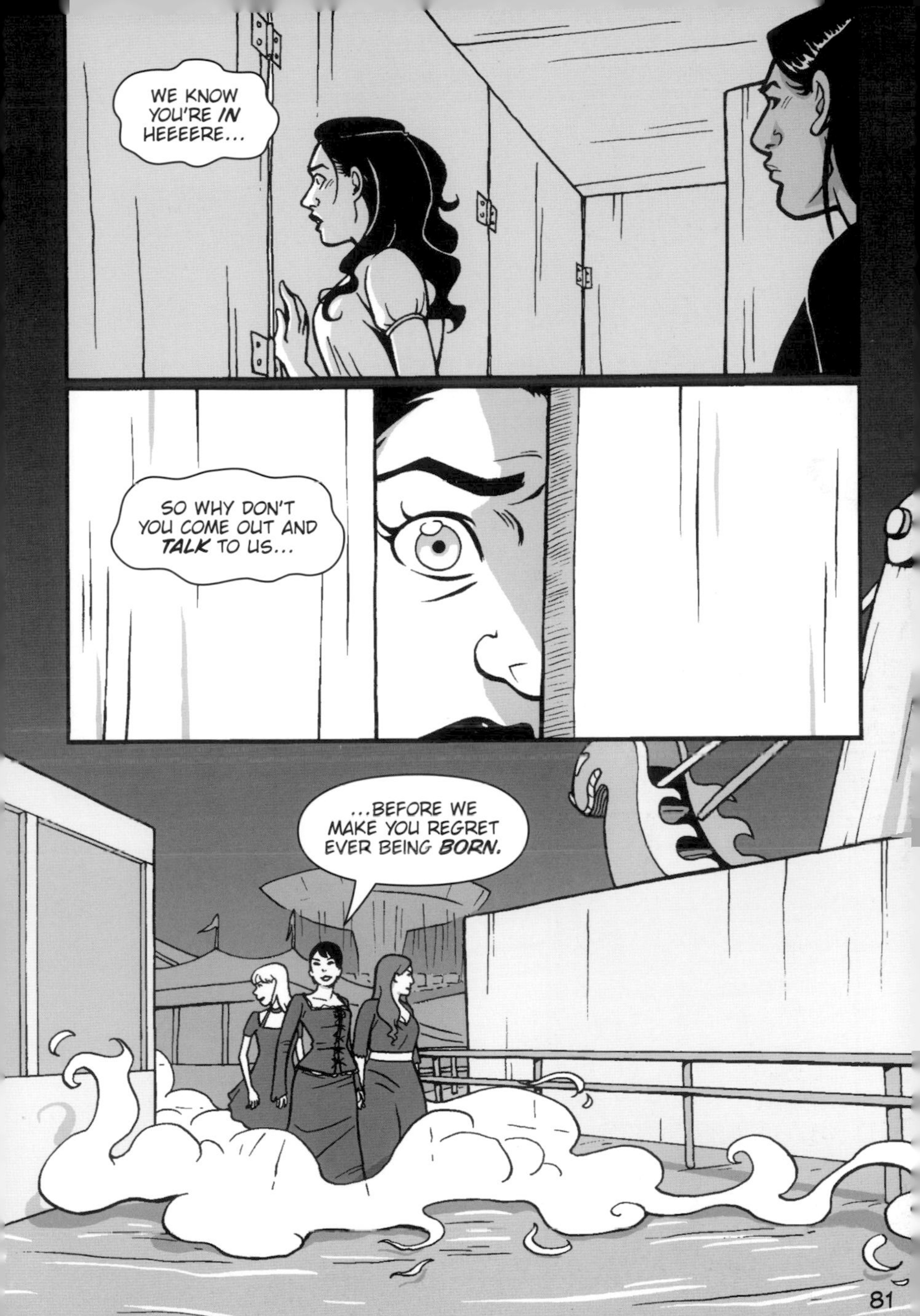
WE KNOW YOU'RE *IN* HEEEERE...
SO WHY DON'T YOU COME OUT AND *TALK* TO US...
...BEFORE WE MAKE YOU REGRET EVER BEING *BORN.*

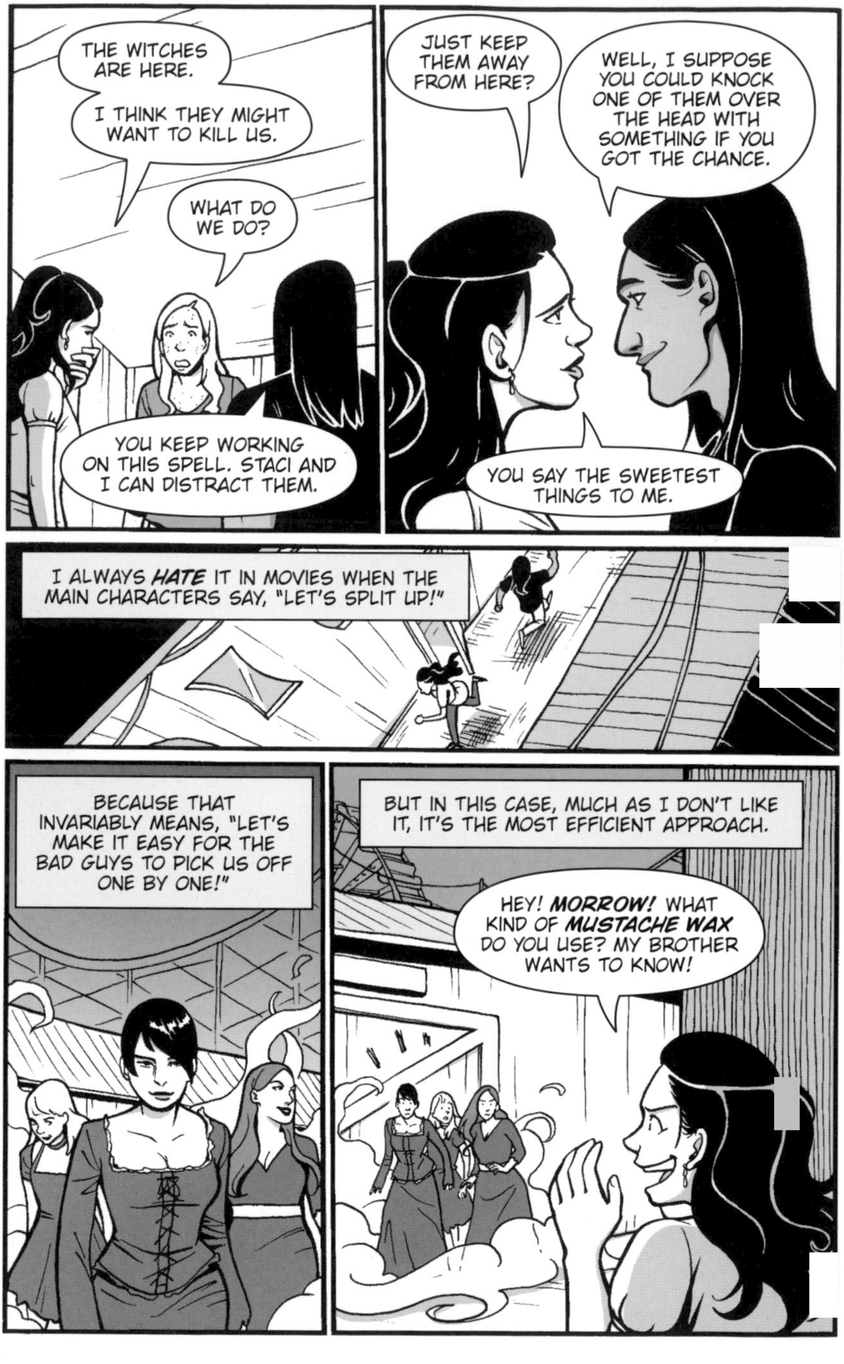
THE WITCHES ARE HERE.
I THINK THEY MIGHT WANT TO KILL US.
WHAT DO WE DO?
YOU KEEP WORKING ON THIS SPELL. STACI AND I CAN DISTRACT THEM.
JUST KEEP THEM AWAY FROM HERE?
WELL, I SUPPOSE YOU COULD KNOCK ONE OF THEM OVER THE HEAD WITH SOMETHING IF YOU GOT THE CHANCE.
YOU SAY THE SWEETEST THINGS TO ME.
I ALWAYS ***HATE*** IT IN MOVIES WHEN THE MAIN CHARACTERS SAY, "LET'S SPLIT UP!"
BECAUSE THAT INVARIABLY MEANS, "LET'S MAKE IT EASY FOR THE BAD GUYS TO PICK US OFF ONE BY ONE!"
BUT IN THIS CASE, MUCH AS I DON'T LIKE IT, IT'S THE MOST EFFICIENT APPROACH.
HEY! ***MORROW!*** WHAT KIND OF ***MUSTACHE WAX*** DO YOU USE? MY BROTHER WANTS TO KNOW!

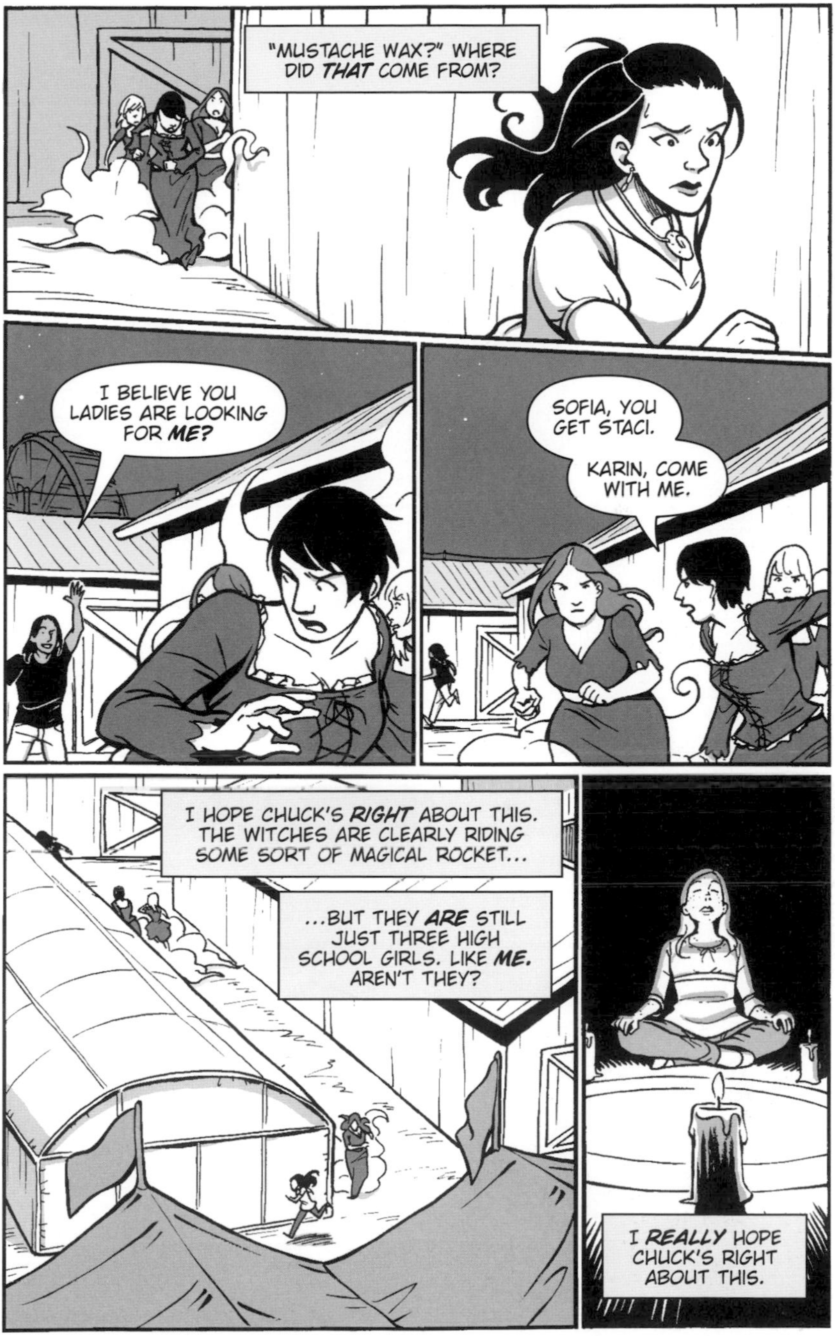
"MUSTACHE WAX?" WHERE DID *THAT* COME FROM?
I BELIEVE YOU LADIES ARE LOOKING FOR *ME?*
SOFIA, YOU GET STACI.
KARIN, COME WITH ME.
I HOPE CHUCK'S *RIGHT* ABOUT THIS. THE WITCHES ARE CLEARLY RIDING SOME SORT OF MAGICAL ROCKET...
...BUT THEY *ARE* STILL JUST THREE HIGH SCHOOL GIRLS. LIKE *ME.* AREN'T THEY?
I *REALLY* HOPE CHUCK'S RIGHT ABOUT THIS.

94

95

CHAPTER FIVE

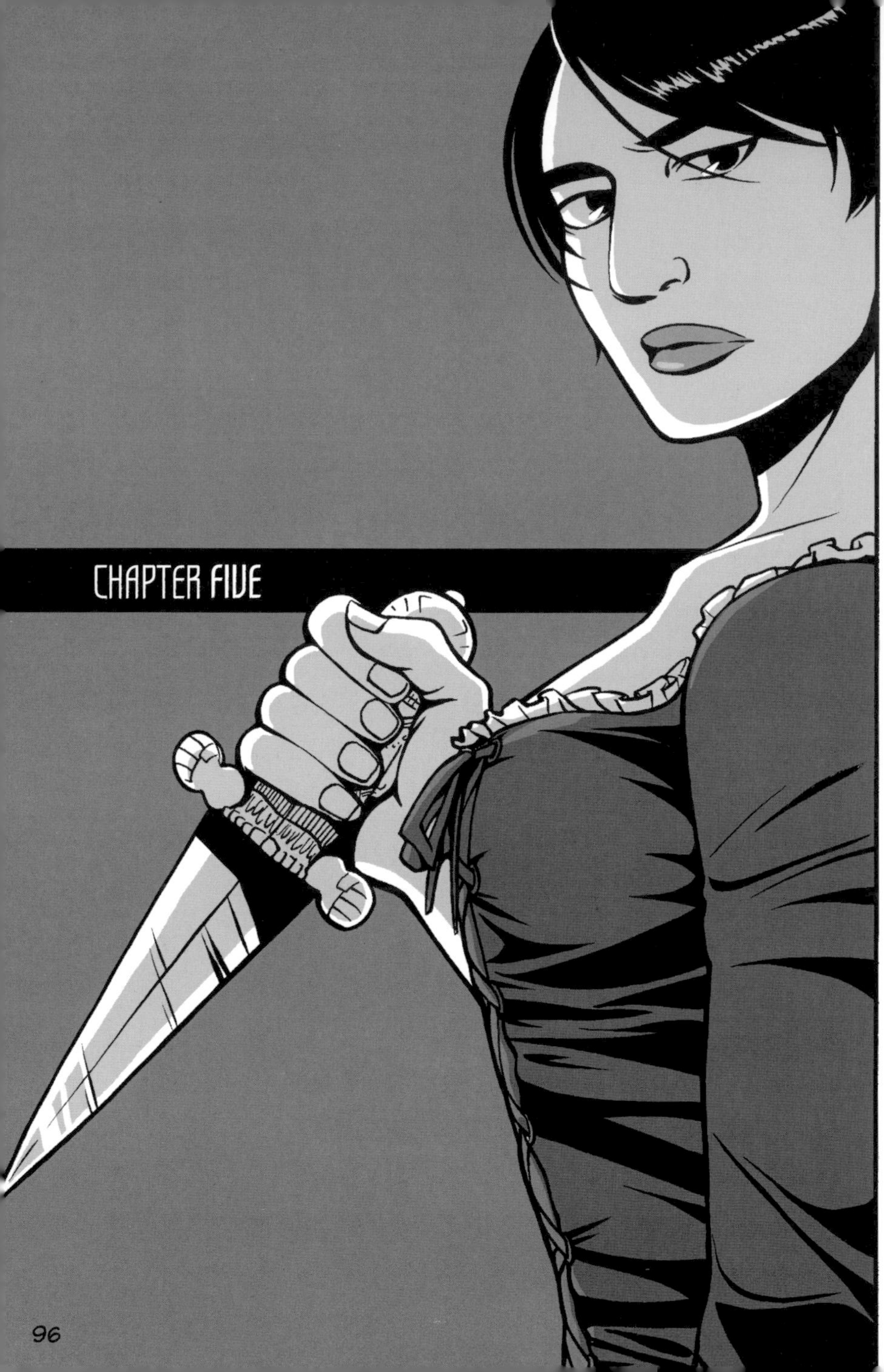

98

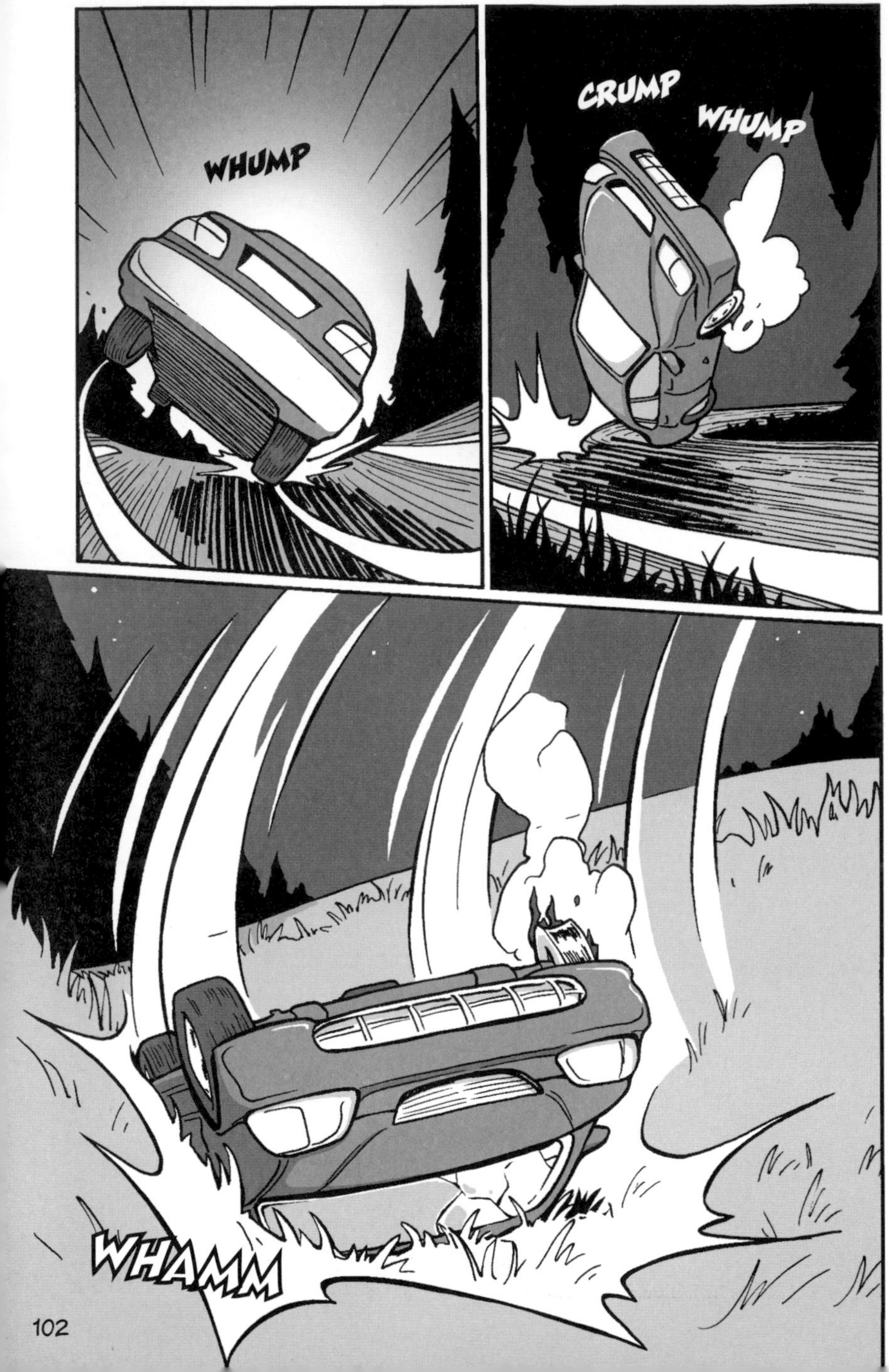
WHUMP
CRUMP
WHUMP
WHAMM

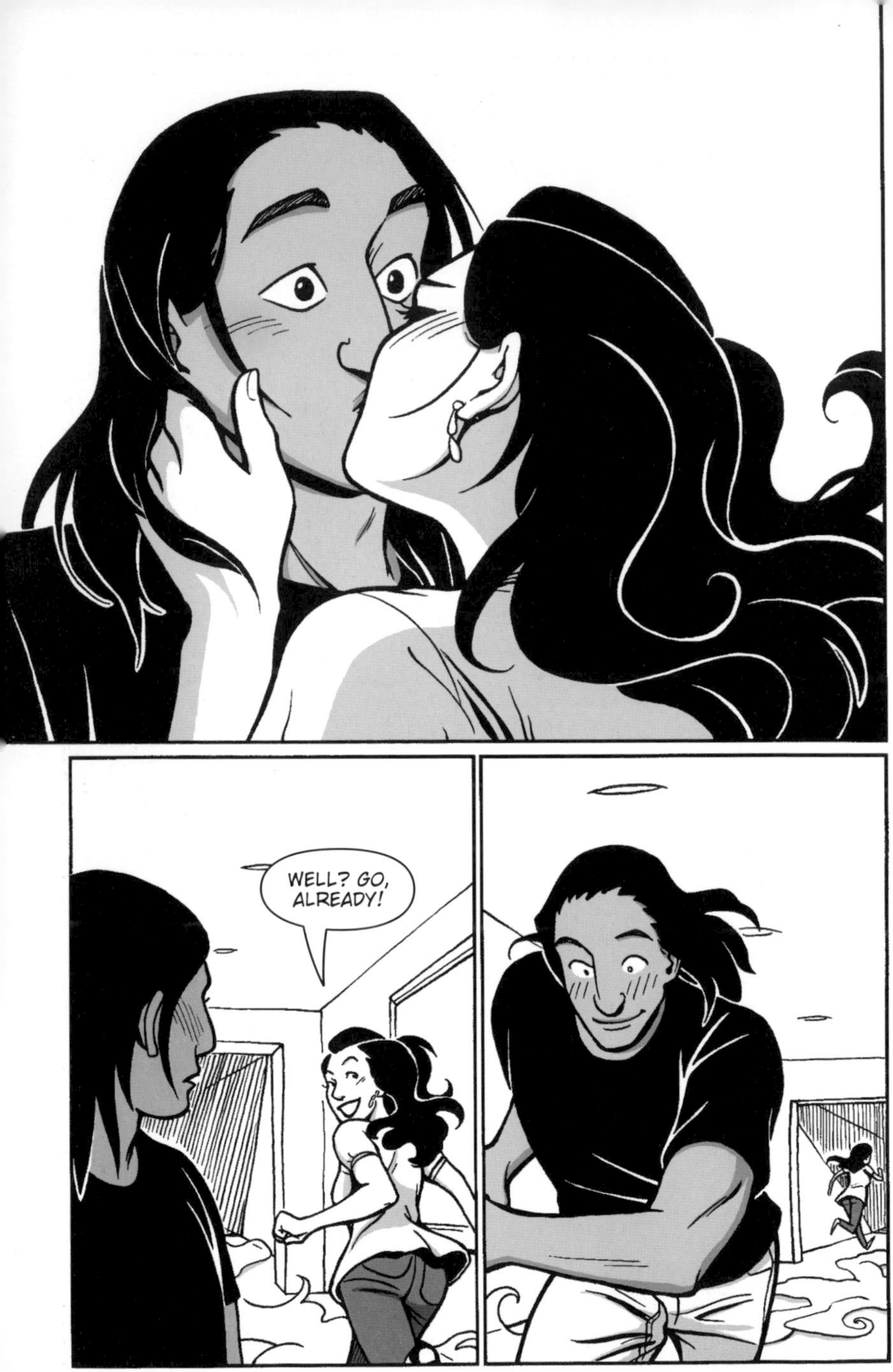
WELL? GO, ALREADY!

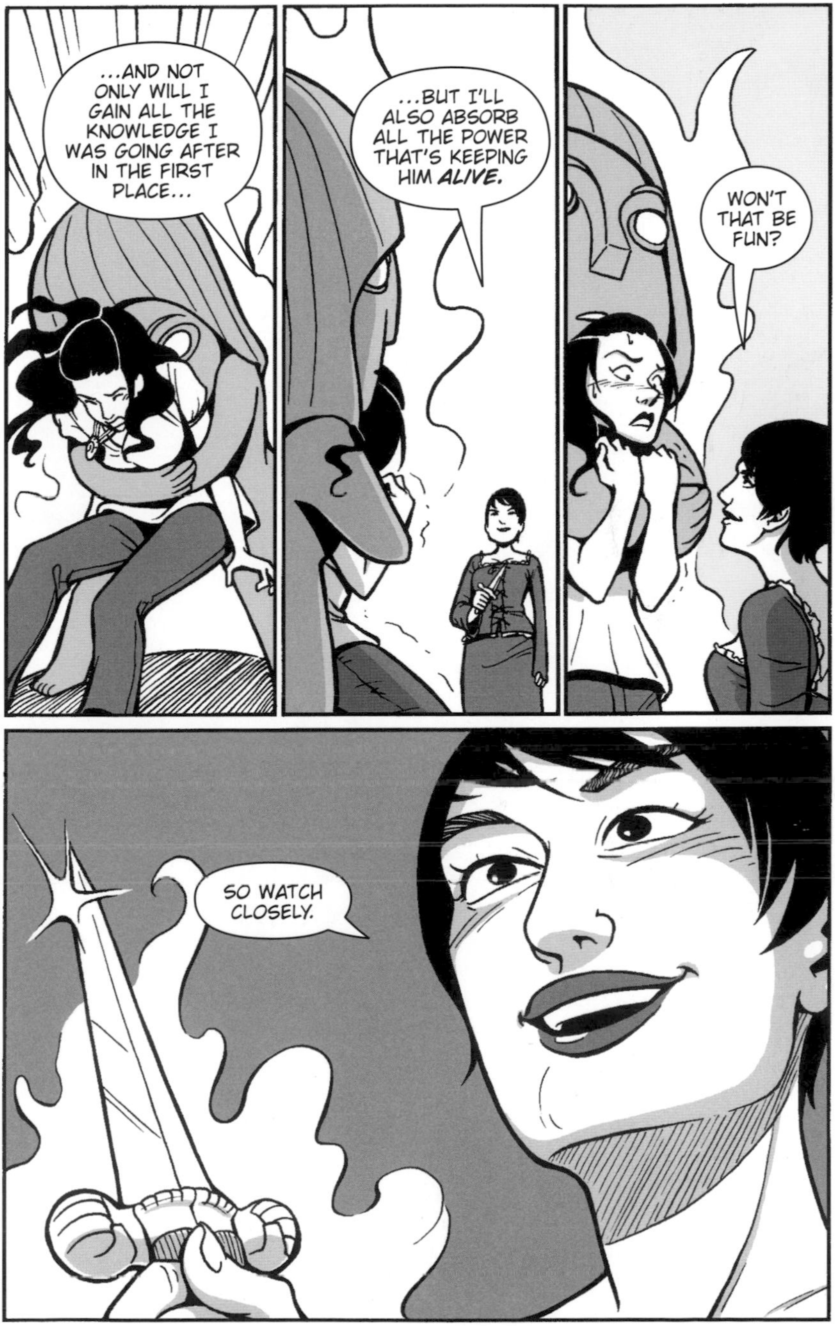
...AND NOT ONLY WILL I GAIN ALL THE KNOWLEDGE I WAS GOING AFTER IN THE FIRST PLACE...
...BUT I'LL ALSO ABSORB ALL THE POWER THAT'S KEEPING HIM *ALIVE.*
WON'T THAT BE FUN?
SO WATCH CLOSELY.

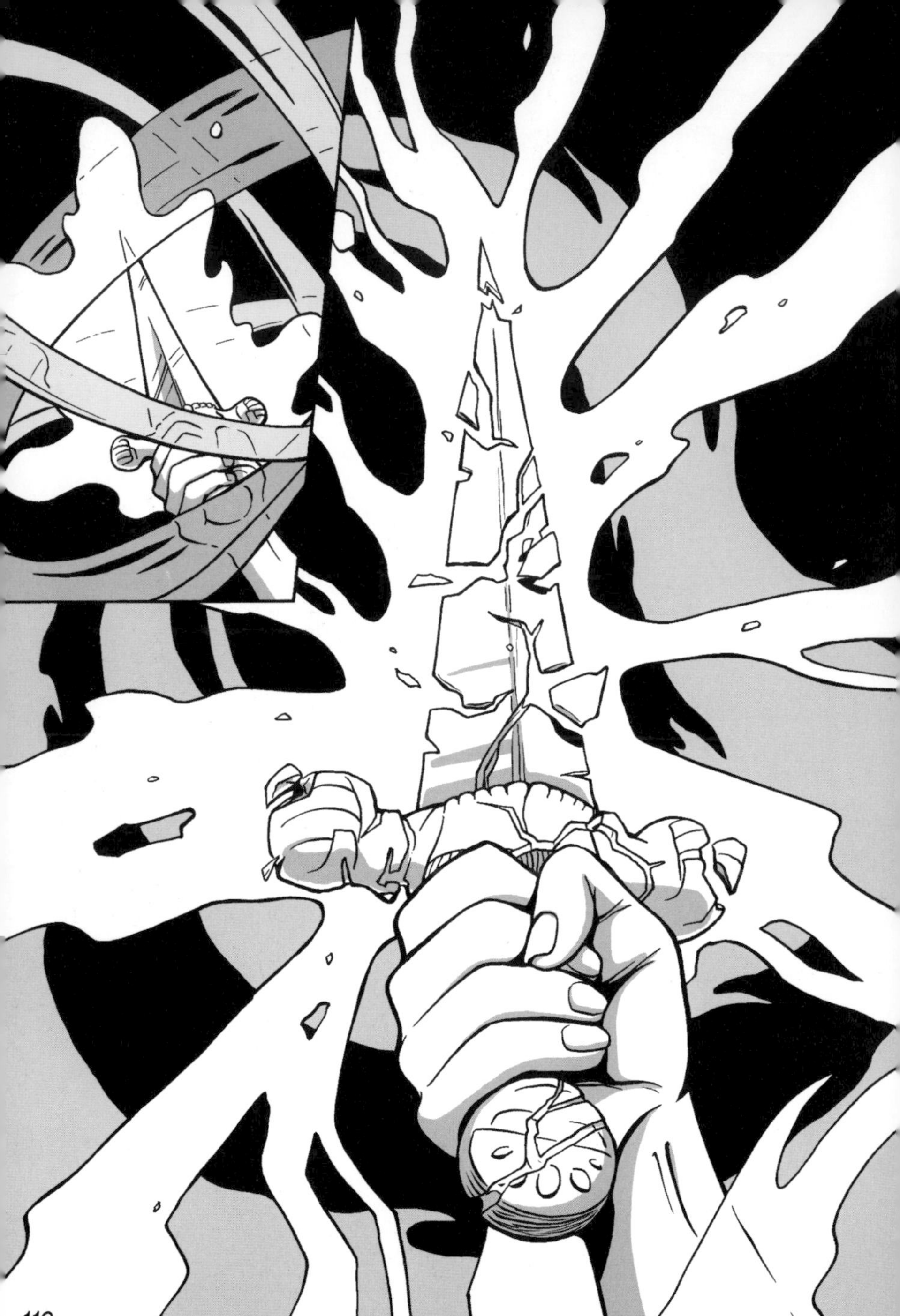

111

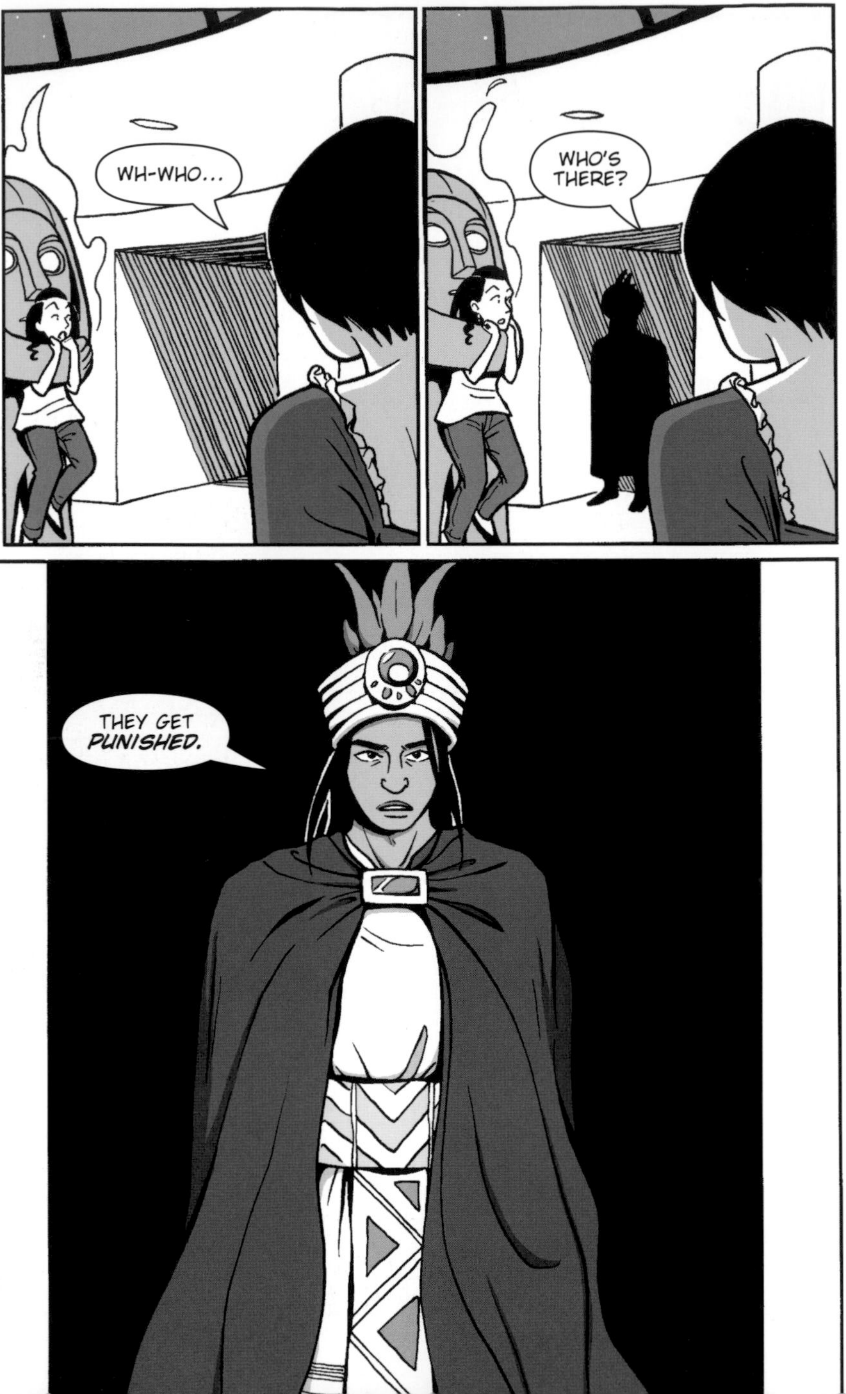
WH-WHO...
WHO'S THERE?
THEY GET *PUNISHED.*

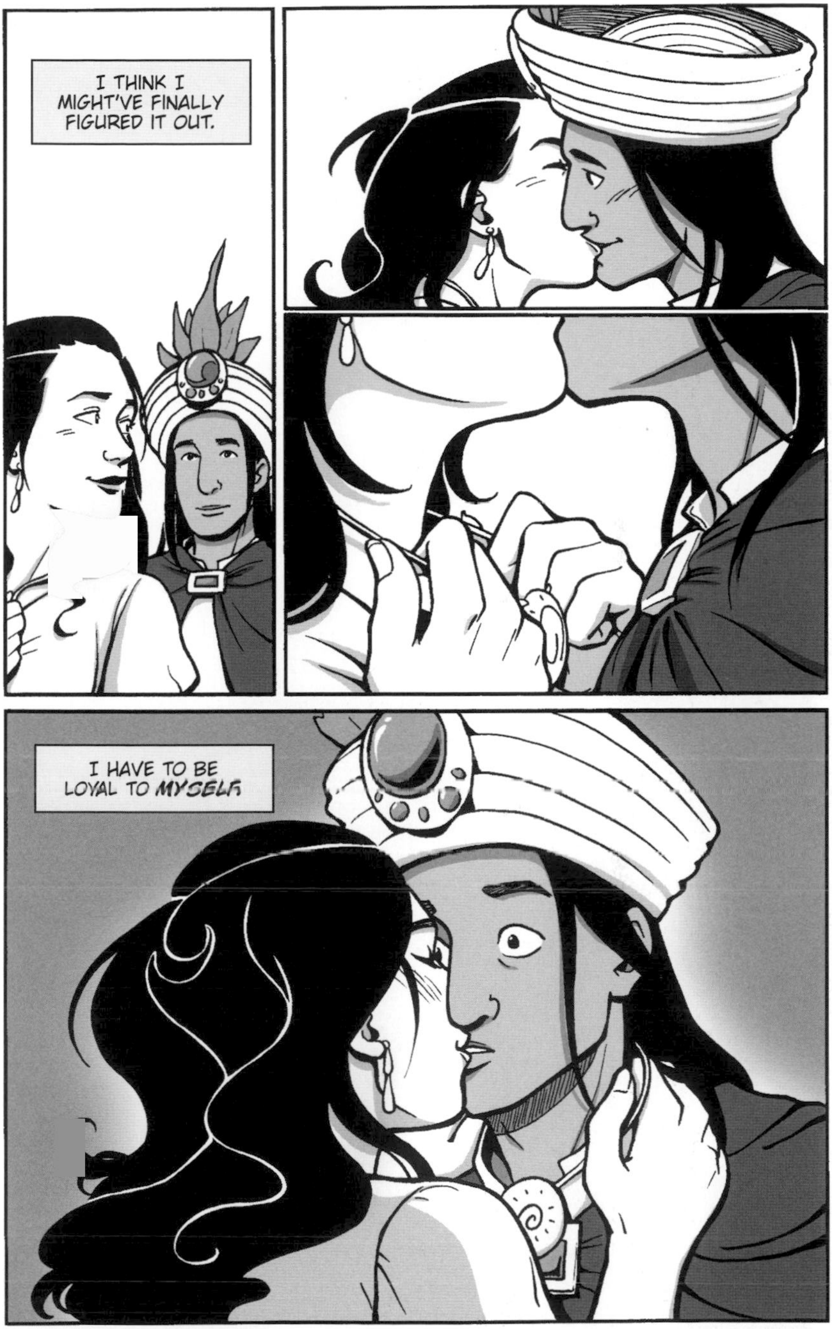
I THINK I MIGHT'VE FINALLY FIGURED IT OUT.
I HAVE TO BE LOYAL TO MYSELF.

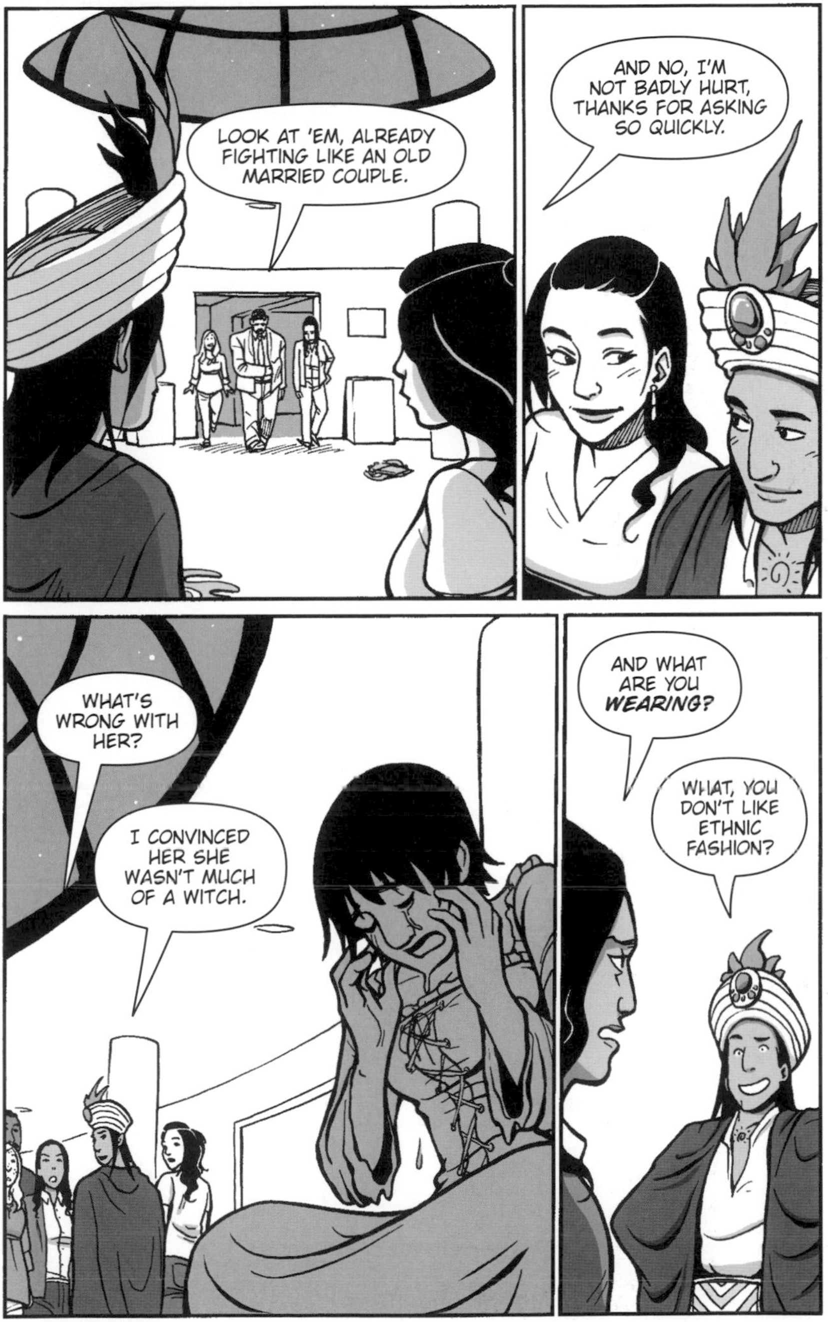
LOOK AT 'EM, ALREADY FIGHTING LIKE AN OLD MARRIED COUPLE.
AND NO, I'M NOT BADLY HURT, THANKS FOR ASKING SO QUICKLY.
WHAT'S WRONG WITH HER?
I CONVINCED HER SHE WASN'T MUCH OF A WITCH.
AND WHAT ARE YOU *WEARING?*
WHAT, YOU DON'T LIKE ETHNIC FASHION?

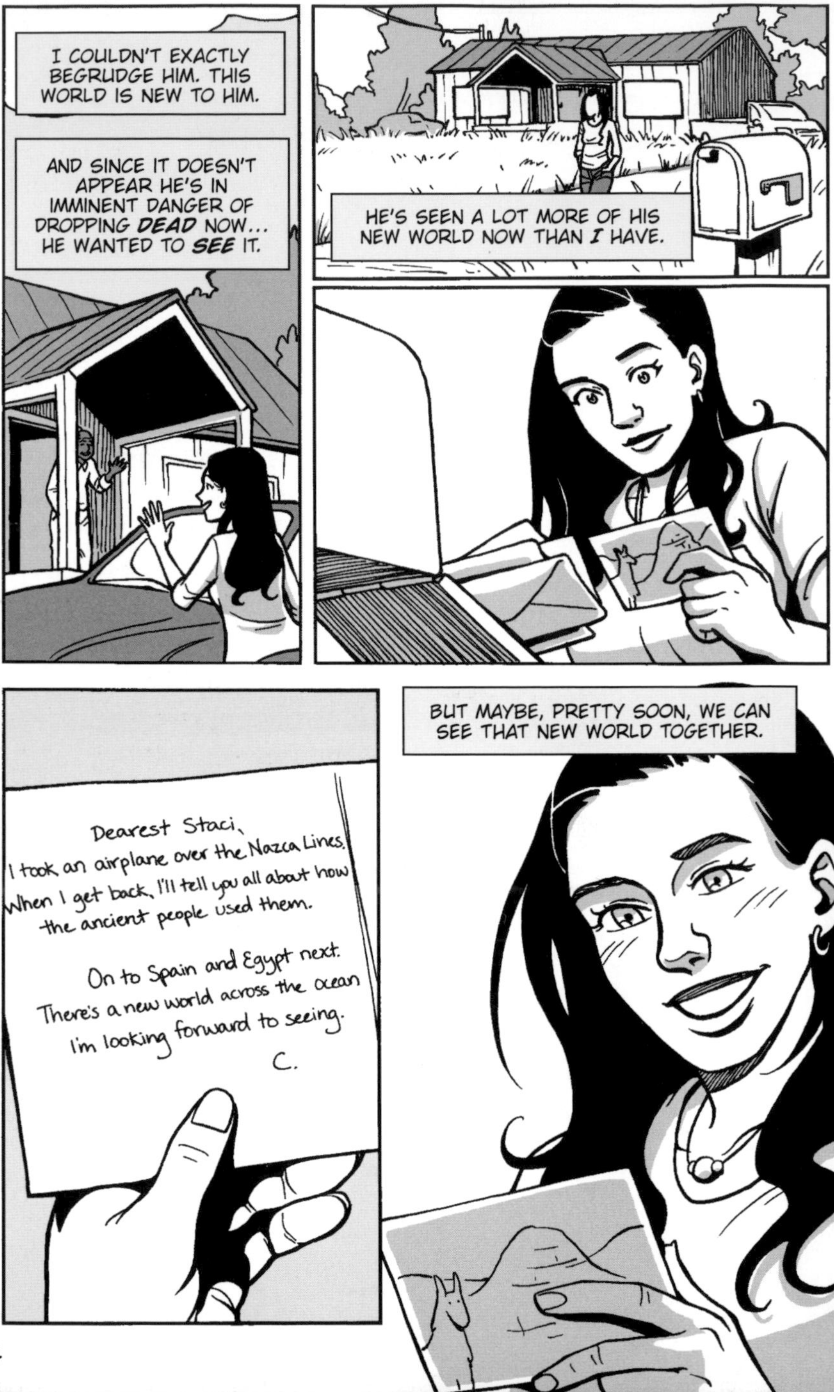
I COULDN'T EXACTLY BEGRUDGE HIM. THIS WORLD IS NEW TO HIM.
AND SINCE IT DOESN'T APPEAR HE'S IN IMMINENT DANGER OF DROPPING *DEAD* NOW... HE WANTED TO *SEE* IT.
HE'S SEEN A LOT MORE OF HIS NEW WORLD NOW THAN *I* HAVE.
Dearest Staci,
I took an airplane over the Nazca Lines.
When I get back, I'll tell you all about how
the ancient people used them.
On to Spain and Egypt next.
There's a new world across the ocean
I'm looking forward to seeing.
C.
BUT MAYBE, PRETTY SOON, WE CAN SEE THAT NEW WORLD TOGETHER.

Q & A WITH PACHACUTEC (AKA CHUCK)

You're from Peru?
I thought mummies came from Egypt!

Most people think that, but since I began my travels, I've learned that mummification has been practiced all over the world. Ancient Egyptians started preserving their dead 5,000 years ago, but they weren't alone. The world's oldest mummies came from my ancient ancestors, the Chinchorros, who lived in southern Peru 7,000 years ago. The Chinchorros did not reserve mummification for the privileged. Everyone, young or old, rich or poor, was mummified. Mummies have also been discovered in Siberia, China, Italy, Australia, Mexico, and many other places. Perhaps the only place mummification hasn't been practiced is Antarctica—which is unfortunate, because preserving the dead would be very simple there!

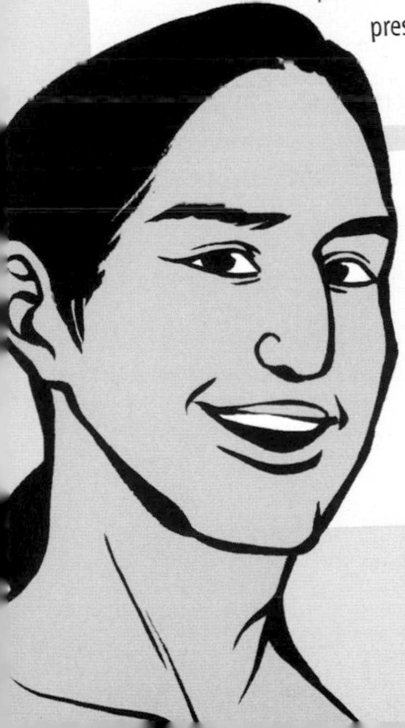

So . . . um, how did you become a mummy? What was it like?

There are two types of mummies: those that are intentionally preserved, like the Egyptian ones you are probably familiar with, and those that were naturally created in environments that are very cold, very dry, or have low oxygen content.

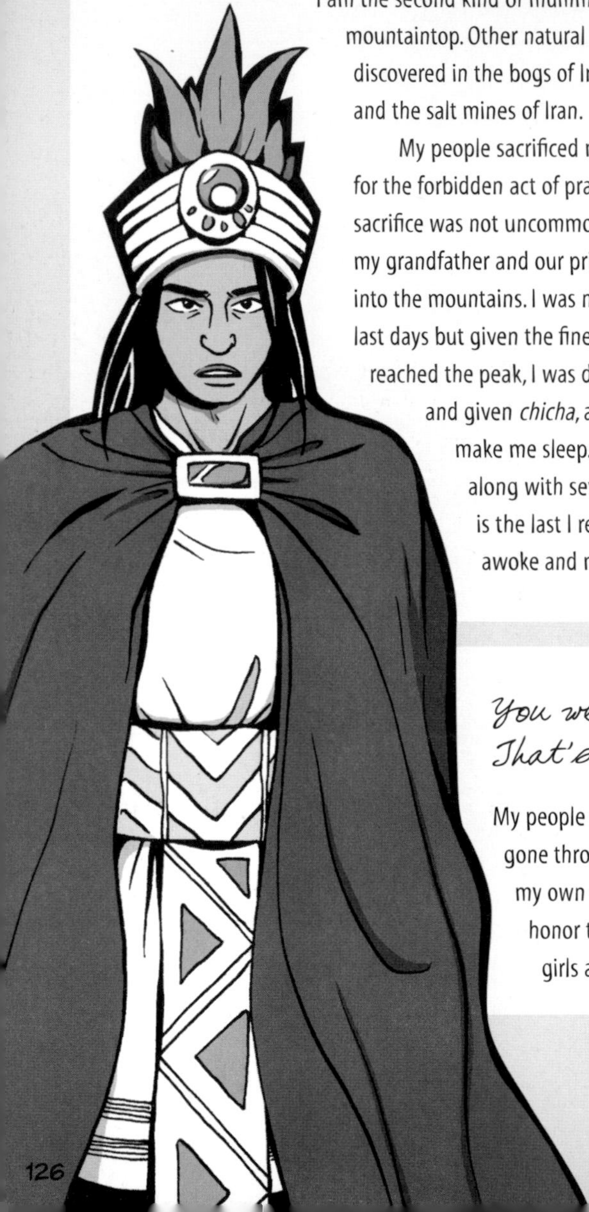

I am the second kind of mummy. I met my end on a frozen mountaintop. Other natural mummies have been discovered in the bogs of Ireland, the deserts of China, and the salt mines of Iran.

My people sacrificed me to the gods, punishment for the forbidden act of practicing magic. Human sacrifice was not uncommon for the Incas. Along with my grandfather and our priests, I made the long trek into the mountains. I was not treated cruelly in those last days but given the finest food to eat. When we reached the peak, I was dressed in my royal clothes and given *chicha*, a fermented corn drink, to make me sleep. I was lowered into a pit along with several precious items. This is the last I remember before the day I awoke and met Staci Glass.

You were sacrificed?
That's so sad.

My people did not think so . . . having gone through the experience, I have my own opinion. It was considered an honor to be given to the gods. Young girls and boys were selected for their beauty and purity—only a prefect specimen would honor the gods. The chosen girls lived a life of comfort and ease in a special temple. They were even escorted to the capital to meet the emperor. Unwilling parents could simply arrange a marriage for their child at an early age, making him or her ineligible for sacrifice.

Were you really a prince?

I was a prince and a warrior, but those honors were taken from me when I used my powers in the heat of battle. An invading army had attacked the capital—I fought while my brother and father fled to the mountains. The day would have been lost had I not used my magic. I transformed the nearby stones into mighty warriors who fended off the intruders. It was my highest moment and perhaps my lowest. My family was displeased, so they made a gift of me to the gods and secretly crowned my brother in my place.

Look in your history book. You'll find the story there (but not the whole story, of course).

ABOUT THE AUTHOR
AND THE ARTIST

Comic book author and video game writer DAN JOLLEY has created work for Marvel, DC, Dark Horse, and TokyoPop and for game developers including Activision and Ubisoft. He is also the author of several Graphic Myths and Legends titles including *Odysseus: Escaping Poseidon's Curse, Pigling: A Cinderella Story,* and *The Hero Twins: Against the Lords of Death.* Among his Twisted Journeys® titles are *Vampire Hunt, Escape from Pyramid X,* and *Agent Mongoose and the Hypno-Beam Scheme.* He wrote *My Boyfriend Bites,* the third book in the My Boyfriend is a Monster series, and also scripts story lines and dialogue for video games such as *Transformers: War for Cybertron* and *Prototype 2.* He lives in Georgia with his wife Tracy and four cats.

NATALIE "TALLY" NOURIGAT is a sequential artist living in Portland, Oregon. She is a member of Periscope Studio and has the pleasure of making comics for a living. Her other comic work includes *Between Gears* (from Image Comics) and *A Boy and a Girl* (from Oni Press).